DOCTOR, DOCTOR

Jake trudged past a sign on a tree, HOME, the letters runny and weathered. He saw Shayla's cabin then, the cold blackness mocking him. Maybe she'd changed her mind.

He followed the direction of the runny arrow, and noticed that the lights in his cabin were on. His footsteps quickened, and he prayed his intruder was tall, beautiful, and could make his heart stop at a hundred paces.

Jake took the stairs in twos and opened the door.

Shayla stood across the room, a fire starter in her hand.

"Hey," he said softly so as not to scare her.

"Hey yourself." The energy she'd come to be known for was gone. "You're all wet. I'll get a towel."

She came back and started rubbing his face with a towel.

"I've missed you," he said.

Her hands slowed. "How much?"

He pulled her at the waist and caught her neck in a tender kiss. Temptation taunted him, but his alter ego issued a stern warning. She was still as soft as he remembered, but not alive the way *his* Shayla had been. He let her go. "Are you staying?" he asked her.

"Ask me to stay."

"Shayla, stay."

"Yes," she whispered.

BOOK YOUR PLACE ON OUR WEBSITE AND MAKE THE ARABESQUE ROMANCE CONNECTION!

We've created a customized website just for our very special Arabesque readers, where you can get the inside scoop on everything that's going on with Arabesque romance novels.

When you come online, you'll have the exciting opportunity to:

- View covers of upcoming books

- Learn about our future publishing schedule (listed by publication month and author)

- Find out when your favorite authors will be visiting a city near you

- Search for and order backlist books

- Check out author bios and background information

- Send e-mail to your favorite authors

- Join us in weekly chats with authors, readers and other guests

- Get writing guidelines

- AND MUCH MORE!

Visit our website at
http://www.arabesquebooks.com

DOCTOR, DOCTOR

Carmen Green

BET Publications, LLC
http://www.bet.com
http://www.arabesquebooks.com

ARABESQUE BOOKS are published by

BET Publications, LLC
c/o BET BOOKS
One BET Plaza
1900 W Place NE
Washington, DC 20018-1211

All Kensington Titles, Imprints, and Distributed Lines are available at special quantity discounts for bulk purchases for sales promotions, premiums, fund-raising, and educational or institutional use. Special book excerpts or customized printings can also be created to fit specific needs. For details, write or phone the office of the Kensington special sales manager: Kensington Publishing Corp., 850 Third Avenue, New York, NY 10022, attn: Special Sales Department, Phone: 1-800-221-2647.

First Printing: May 2002
10 9 8 7 6 5 4 3 2 1

Printed in the United States of America

Thank you, Lord.
This book is dedicated to Gwen Osborne, who loves the
Crawfords, and never let me forget that I love them too.

One

"Have you lost your mind?"

Twenty-five-year-old Shayla Michaels-Crawford stared pitifully at her father, and for one brief moment wanted to scream, "Yes."

Maybe if she pled insanity, her parents would forgive her momentary lapse in judgment and overlook the broken furniture and shattered porcelain figurines.

Maybe if she claimed to have temporarily lost her mind, they'd chalk up her irresponsible behavior to one last fling of fun before real life began.

She could argue that she'd hardly had time to party while a resident at Atlanta General Hospital, and now that she was done, this had been her last hurrah.

And when they would finally see things for what they really were, she'd end by telling them this entire incident wasn't really her fault.

Acquaintances of friends of friends, two women, were the idiots who got into a fight over a man. Shayla couldn't believe they'd acted so juvenile, but it had been fun to antagonize the catfight—Jack Daniels and Coca-Cola made things funny—until things started breaking.

Shayla looked at the room through her father's eyes. The creamy leather love seat leaned sadly to one side, the leg snapped in the frenzy of weave pulling and ripped halters.

The middle cushion sagged, victimized by red wine and blood.

If the room looked half as bad to her father as it did to her, she was in major trouble. Shayla recalled the last time her father had given her that "how could you do this?" look.

She'd been nineteen and had taken his Mercedes out for a joyride. She'd wrecked it, taking the corner of Old Alabama too fast, and had broken three ribs and the entire front end for her trouble.

Her dad had been relieved she was alive, but the disappointment on his face slapped a lid on her rebellious nature, and allowed her to begin the process of forgiving him for not being in her life.

"Dad, this is a terrible misunderstanding," she told him now, hoping to distract his wide-eyed, shocked stare.

"You'd better believe it is, because this is a home, not a playground for overage adolescents!" Rage painted his eyes the color of wet cement. "What was going through your mind?"

"Noth—" she started.

"Did I say speak?"

The words dived down her throat along with any hope of redemption. Shayla dragged the broom across the now worthless garbage and froze when the severed head of one of her mother's prized Lladro angels rolled to a stop at her toes.

Her father stooped and picked up the broken cherub. "I've been telling you for the past year that you needed to grow up and get your act together, but you claimed you needed a break."

Her father's voice tripped her anger. What was he so upset about? At least this time she hadn't broken three ribs! "Do you know how exhausting residency is, Dad? It's ten times harder than when you went to med school." The argument had sounded fine before it was completely out of her mouth, but now Shayla felt as if a pendulum of doom had suddenly knocked her in the head.

"Really?"

Eric Crawford's sudden conversational reply welcomed a convincing argument.

"Ninety percent of my colleagues took a minimum of a month off. They went to the Riviera, Asia, and even Africa, but not me. I stayed home to hang out with you and Mom. And what do I get for my thoughtfulness? A hard time over a few broken objects." She gave him a disappointed shake of her head.

"So that's how you justify what happened here."

Shayla swiped the broom under the raised end of the couch.

"No." The word slipped into a cry of regret as the wing of the headless angel flew out and hit her father's leg.

He didn't say anything as he bent slowly and picked up the piece, but a vein throbbed at his temple. "How old are you?"

"Twenty-five." Shayla had never feared her father, but today she was afraid their relationship, which had been mostly of him giving and her taking, had just turned a corner.

The dispassionate look on his face was something

she'd never seen before. If only he'd returned the day after tomorrow as planned, the housekeepers she'd ordered early this morning would have come and cleaned up all the evidence of the party from hell.

And Shayla would have emptied her meager savings and replaced every statue with a brand-new one.

"Twenty-five." Eric Crawford repeated her, and his gaze trailed across the broken glass table that now leaned against the stone base. "You did better when you were a teenager."

"Dad, it looks worse than it is."

His expression changed to thoughtful until he bent down again. He'd found the angel's harp. Shayla backed up at the dangerous glint in his eyes.

"No, it doesn't. It is what it is. You've lost your fool mind." He shoved his hands at her, the broken pieces falling to her feet. "I was wrong," he admitted to himself. "And your mother was right. I should have made you go to work at the office right away. But no, I was soft."

The words curled from his lips with such disbelief she wanted to fall at his feet and beg him to go away for a day so she could make things better. "I can fix this, Daddy."

She began to sweep in earnest. Meat from a submarine sandwich caught on the broom and smeared mayonnaise on the wooden floor. Shayla thought it best to stop moving.

"No, you can't. You've proven you need help growing up."

"Dad, I agree, I should suffer consequences."

"You better believe it."

"This mess will be cleaned up in no time." Shayla leaned the broom against the wall and adjusted the fern that leaned awkwardly in a vase her parents had picked up while touring China.

Normally, Shayla would've left the plant alone, but with her dad watching, she had no choice but to adjust it so it sat flat.

She plunged her hand into the dirt along the side. When it hit an odd shape, she pulled. "Dad, I'm as disappointed as you. Really," she said, striving to sound mature. "I'll supervise everything. You can go on to bed and by the time you get up, it'll be like nothing happened."

"How generous of you."

"I knew you'd understand." Shayla gave her father a disarming smile and pulled once more. A pint-size liquor bottle pulled out, unwrapped, unused condoms glued on as eyes. A raggedly torn ring from an opened condom formed the mouth, but the low-hanging, fully extended condom nose brought her father several feet off the floor.

"I—I—I. I'm sorry. I'll make this up to you."

"That's it! Oh—" He laughed and Shayla put the sofa between them. He walked and talked to himself. "I'm going to do what I always do. I'm going to fix this. You're going to pay for this."

"Pay?" she asked, indignant. She never expected her father to really drain her savings account. "You mean with money?"

"To start with, yes."

"Dad, that's what insurance is for. Besides, it was just a party that got a bit out of control. Let's not blow this out of proportion."

"I'm kicking you out."

The words were so low and lethal, Shayla froze. In her brain, she hit the rewind button. Air rushed into her lungs fast and she coughed to get it out. She couldn't have heard right. *Kick her out?*

Had he lost *his* mind? "That's right. On the midnight train out of Georgia."

Shayla wondered if her father had suffered a breakdown or something. He only quoted old songs when he was in a nostalgic or an angry mood. "You're outta here. On the first thing smoking to Mississippi."

"What's in Mississippi?" she demanded.

"A quaint medical facility that needs an interim doctor. If you want to have a future in medicine, you'll report to work Monday at the Alberta Medical Center in Alberta, Mississippi."

She'd never heard of the obscure town, or the off-the-map storefront doctor's office. The idea twisted her nose.

"I'm joining the family practice," she enunciated clearly. "In September."

"Over my dead body," her father said.

"I know this looks bad and yes, I've been relaxing too much. Okay? But banishment to Nowhereville, USA, isn't fair."

"You don't get it, do you?"

Shayla wiped her French-manicured fingertips on a napkin.

"You think I'm immature, and by the looks of things, I'd think that also. But, when I come on board in September, I'll be one hundred percent."

She hurried over to the rack of her father's CD collection, and wished they hadn't gotten caught in the brawl. Joe Sample, Pieces of a Dream, and George Howard had been crushed, the silver disks splintered like the skin around an old woman's eyes. She tucked them into the garbage bag.

"I'm not paying for your student loan."

Suddenly the threat of Mississippi made sense.

Shayla had taken out the tiny loan while her mother had been on her European singing tour. She and her best friend Caitlin Rogers had wanted to join friends in Aruba. But that was five years ago. Shayla had forgotten all about the Goldwyn program. "Dad, it was only seven thousand dollars," she reasoned. "What is everyone going to think of me? All of my colleagues are in private practice or have taken positions with the top hospitals in the nation. I'm an *Emory University graduate*! You can keep my first paycheck, okay?" she offered.

"Not only am I not paying off your loan, if you don't report to the Alberta center, I'll have your license suspended."

Shayla couldn't believe her father would hurt her like this. "Why won't you forgive me?"

"Because, my darling, you're a selfish, spoiled adult. It's partially my fault. And, you don't know how to apologize. My brothers and I used to have a saying, 'if you're bad enough to pick a fight with a big dog, you'd better know how to bite.' It's time you learn how the real world works."

Her eyes stung. "You'd be ruining my life. Can you live with that?"

His sad look didn't come close to the torment she felt.

"I'm giving you a chance to become the responsible woman I know you can be. Your commitment will be satisfied April first, next year." Eric headed for the stairs. "If this place isn't cleaned and you're gone by eight A.M., you'll be sorry."

"But—"

"Nothing," he finished.

"Dad, I'm sorry."

He crossed and kissed her forehead, but stepped away before she could embrace him and beg. "Good night."

Shayla sank to the floor. Alberta, Mississippi. Where was that? Between Natchez and nowhere, Caitlin had said when they'd subsidized their vacation.

Shayla placed both hands on the floor and yelped as shards of glass pierced her palms. "Fine." She grabbed the broom and cried as she cleaned. Finally the house was restored. Then she packed until dawn.

If her father wanted her gone, she'd leave and prove she could make it on her own. She packed the car, then ravaged the Subzero refrigerator.

As she walked through the foyer, glistening in the dewy early morning light, Shayla took one last look around and vowed not to return until her parents came to their senses.

TWO

Shayla guided her car deep into the valley of the Delta.

Cedars, cypresses, Carolina sapphires, and spruce trees lined the highway on both sides, broken by acres of cotton. She hadn't seen a person since the gas station attendant over an hour ago. No sane human dared go where she was going.

A knot of resentment exploded in her stomach. Shayla still couldn't believe her parents. She'd heard the tail end of her father's conversation, his defense of Damon, and his laughter.

At seventeen, Shayla had inadvertently met the biological father she'd never known. When he and her adoptive mother had fallen in love and married, they'd developed a bond even Shayla couldn't penetrate. She'd been jealous of their love, her mother having been her world until then.

But a twist of fate had brought father and daughter

together, and the families had blended. Within the space of a beating heart, she'd become a daughter, niece, granddaughter, and cousin.

She'd become a Crawford, and all the trappings of the Crawford name became an unshakable cloak. Sometimes she'd been honored she was a member of a large, wealthy family that helped influence the leadership, law, and medical communities of Atlanta.

But other times she'd wanted to be regular and cut-up like some of her friends.

For so long, Lauren Michaels and Shayla's Grandmother Chaney had been the center of her world. But the Crawfords had welcomed them all into the fold.

What would the family think of what her father had done?

Would her grandfather send her uncles after her? This did qualify as cruel and unusual punishment.

The scenery blended into a green glob of uniformity that reminded Shayla of strained baby peas. How many deaths in the state of Mississippi were attributed to boredom?

She slowed and checked the directions again.

The gas station attendant had told her to go forty miles west, look for the fruit stand, then veer right. Keep straight 2.2 miles, take a left onto the gravel road, and down about half a mile was the driveway leading to the center. But if she missed the right turn, she'd have to travel another five miles before the road split and she could turn around.

Speedometer at fifty, Shayla coasted, looking for the fruit stand. *What if the fruit stand man died?* She thought and laughed. *It'd be just my luck.*

She rolled past a well-manicured complex of buildings that rose in modern architecture against the darkening sky. Her heart skipped a beat in relief. There was civilian life out here.

Twenty miles turned into thirty and she saw a lonely man sitting beneath an umbrella, the trunk of his hatchback open.

No stand, though. He waved and she waved back, but kept going.

The radio fuzzed and Shayla turned off the annoyance. She hadn't left Atlanta until noon, trying to think of a way to convince her father he'd been too harsh. But every argument had been reinforced by his words. *You're spoiled rotten. And you don't know how to apologize.* Her mind protested, but he hadn't answered the phone when she'd called. Her mother hadn't either. None of the uncles had answered their phones, nor her grandparents. Shayla felt all alone.

Her bladder expanded and she yawned. She needed a couch, fast.

Relief hit her like a well-placed slap on the back. *I don't have to sleep on a couch anymore, I'm a real doctor.*

The glow disappeared as the road cruised toward an embankment of trees and split.

Where was the fruit stand?

Tears blurred her vision, so she pulled over, shut off the engine, and rested her head on the steering wheel.

Why is this happening to me? Shayla indulged the sniffles, then lifted her head and let out a bloodcurdling scream.

A black bear stared through the windshield at her.

Shayla scrambled toward the backseat, unable to find refuge between her bags of luggage. Her neck burned from the seat belt and she screamed until she saw stars.

The bear walked toward the driver's side.

He tilted his head, looking annoyed that she was disrupting his peace. He growled and pushed the car, then crossed the road and disappeared into the woods.

Gulping, Shayla sobbed. This was completely her father's fault. He had to know her life was in danger. After he heard about the bear, he would come to his senses. She had no choice.

In the debris on the passenger seat, she found her cell phone and pressed his preprogrammed number, only to get a busy signal.

He wasn't even home to save her.

She had to get to the Alberta Medical Center before it was pitch-black out, or she might never be heard from again.

Shayla started the car and drove back to the spot where she'd seen the man. He was gone, but she turned anyway, following the meticulous directions until she drove up to a gray, one-story building, surrounded by overgrown trees and a partially graveled lot.

The building reminded Shayla of one of the condemned structures the Atlanta Housing Commissioners tore down with regularity. Support beams might aid the leaning double-wide building, but a match and gasoline were the better choice.

Her headlights bounced off a crudely sketched message that hung askew from the doorknob. WELCOME TO HELL.

Shayla's mouth dropped open. What? These hillbillies must be out of their minds.

Fatigue transformed into stubborn will. She might be in purgatory for the next 364 days, but she wasn't taking anybody's crap while she was there.

Lightning bugs, mosquitoes, and moths swam outside in the glow of an indoor yellow light. Shayla gathered her purse, keys, and cell phone, then reached for the handle.

Two sharp raps against the driver's window sent Shayla screaming into the passenger seat.

A face appeared in the window. "Doctor Crawford?"

Shayla tried to calm herself. "Who are you?"

The man outside the car tried the door. "Would you like to get out?"

"Who are you?" she shouted, and hated the fear in her voice. This was Mississippi. A land so foreign it might as well have been Jupiter. She didn't know the man with the mean brown eyes and the frowning mouth.

All she knew was that if he decided to come through the window, her finger was perched on the trigger of some pepper spray with his name on it.

"I'm Doctor Jake Parker. Are you getting out?"

He seemed angry, as if her fear offended him. He wasn't from Atlanta. He didn't know "the rules." Men didn't just talk to her. In her circle of friends, men were introduced. And they never knocked on car windows.

Shayla gathered her scattered belongings and got out on the passenger side of the car.

Jake Parker looked off into the distance as if searching for an answer—or maybe, another doctor. The thought made her angry.

Who was he to judge her? She didn't need attitude from a doctor who probably got his degree through the mail. When he finally looked at her again, her first reaction was to get into her car, turn around, and go home. She could always be a pharmacist.

But med school had taught her more than just medicine. She'd learned perseverance. She'd learned to work with arrogant men who thought they ruled the world.

At the moment, Jake didn't look any different from them.

"I'm out. Happy?"

"I thought you might have been a patient, but your Georgia tags gave you away."

"Obviously." Shayla stayed on her side of the car, talking over the roof. "Thank you for waiting, Doctor Parker. If you'll tell me where my apartment is, I'll get settled in and meet you back here in the morning."

The headlights on her BMW shifted off, casting them into darkness. Shayla couldn't help her sharp intake of breath. She swatted at bugs and dropped her purse and keys. She reached to get them and saw something slither across her shoes. A scream tore from her throat and Doctor Parker laughed.

Shayla had never hated anyone, but Jake Parker was easily going to be the first.

He flipped on a flashlight and the bugs swam over.

"Do you want to get your bags?" he said.

"No, I'll just drive over. Where do I live?"

"That's going to be a problem."

"Why?" she asked, annoyed and more than a little impatient.

"Might not be a problem for you, though. You look strong enough."

"What do your patients call you?" she asked.

"Doctor Parker. Why?"

"Doctor Death might be more appropriate."

She could see his smile in silhouette. "Why?"

"Because if you take as much time giving a diagnosis as it's taking you to give me directions, your patients should all be dead!"

He came around the car and shoved the flashlight into her hand. He looked mean again. Shayla was too tired to care.

"All right, Doctor Crawford, I can see we're already going to have problems. You can't drive to your cabin because the road's been washed out for a week. Take that path over there until it dead-ends. On the right twenty yards in is your cabin. We start at seven. Welcome to Alberta."

He walked opposite her path, and was swallowed up by the midnight sky and deep green trees. How far was she to walk? A mile, two? Were there lights on in her cabin? Who was going to help her with her bags? She couldn't leave them.

Shayla felt her chin trembling. But she wouldn't cry. This was the hand she'd been dealt. She was going to live with it, but she was damned if she was walking through anybody's woods to an uncertain end. What if the bear came back?

She sniffed and clutched the flashlight.

This could be *Blair Witch*, she thought and slapped a mosquito on her neck. Instead, she forced herself to quickly find her keys and purse. Shayla crawled into her car, locked the doors, lowered the seat, and went to sleep.

Three

Jake Parker awoke with Shayla on his mind.

He hit the trail for his weekly run that took him through growing Christmas trees, up four and a half miles, and onto the rarely used Geronimo trails.

Jake loved the time alone with nobody tugging at him or filling his mind with problems. This time was for his thoughts, his peace, and he took it as often as possible.

His sneakers crunched against dirt and stones as he raced to capture his natural rhythm. He tried not to think about the day ahead, but couldn't help it. Today wasn't going to be easy.

Dr. Shayla Crawford wasn't what any of them had expected.

She wasn't meek or humble or even afraid. She was there. Like a splash of red on a white canvas.

She was going to get on his staff's nerves. Especially Pearline's.

Jake's side pinched as he detoured, heading toward

the river, needing the familiarity to center him. Everything was changing again. Spring had brought forth color to the dull winter branches and he loved how spring made him feel.

The landscape he'd loved from childhood burst with vitality, the smell of the forest intoxicating his troubled mind. This was his time, he reminded himself. *No worries.*

Like the transmission on a car, he finally hit his stride and his body settled into a comfortable glide. Jake stretched his legs, full stride, wishing he could fly. But that was a child's fantasy. Just like saving his mother from breast cancer.

Jake rounded a curve and his ankle turned right as his body went left. He pitched forward and fell.

Brambles caught on his T-shirt, his elbows meeting rock as he rolled. Too late he stuck out his hands, right before his knee slammed into a boulder.

He came to an abrupt stop and grabbed his leg. Fiery spears of pain shot through his knee, making him wince as he limped to his feet. His neck prickled and Jake took the warning seriously and turned slowly.

A black bear, twenty feet away, sized him up.

The animal looked between two and three years of age, but was already as tall as Jake, and two hundred pounds heavier.

Jake inched backward.

The bear moved closer.

Jake froze. He hadn't seen a black bear in about ten years. Their numbers had dwindled dangerously low, but this one was not only young, but curious.

Jake bled from the knees and hands. Black bears weren't carnivorous by nature, but their acute sense of smell could get Jake killed. He settled his eyes below the bear's neck and slowly stooped and picked up two rocks.

The bear tilted his head and ambled his bulky frame forward. Jake threw the first rock and hit the bear's stomach, falling like a badly thrown shot put.

The bear merely grunted.

He ambled again, and Jake threw the other rock, this time giving a yell to scare him off. But the bear wasn't deterred and sauntered forward again.

Fear gripped Jake and he panicked, stumbling backward. Not only was the smell of blood and human sweat attractive to the beast, but so was fear. The bear advanced.

A gunshot split the air, and whizzed past the bear's head. The animal turned and growled.

Jake put the thigh-high boulder between them and looked out the other side.

Shayla Crawford stood at the crest of the clearing, Jake's rifle cocked, loaded, and aimed at the bear's heart.

The bear considered her for a moment and she fired again, this time her intent clear.

The hulking animal dropped to his paws and Shayla cocked the gun again.

The bear had had enough. He ran into the woods and didn't look back.

Jake's heart hammered. His body ached. His pride stung.

Dr. Crawford hadn't relaxed her stance, but her gaze shifted from the woods to him. "Can you make it back?"

"Yes." His breath burst from his chest in great gulps. He looked down to inspect his injuries and determined he'd live.

Shayla Crawford had saved his life.

Shayla Crawford had his gun. Jake looked up. Shayla Crawford was gone.

He'd just stared into the face of a black bear and had

been rescued by Dr. Shayla Crawford. How had she found him? How had she gotten his rifle?

As a just-in-case, Jake gathered more rocks and walked home. When he entered his house, he stopped cold.

Suitcases were open all over the floor, garments strewn from one end of the furniture to the other. A madwoman had ransacked his house.

"Doctor Crawford." Jake stepped over silk and satin, leather and lace, labels he didn't recognize on the clothes.

They all smelled like dry cleaning solvent and money.

A dress bag of suits lay against the couch, gaping open. What in the hell would possess her to come into his home?

Jake maneuvered to the short hallway, and encountered a locked bathroom door. He hammered with his fist and winced. "Doctor Crawford, what are you doing here?"

The door snapped open and Jake took a step back.

Shayla Crawford was drop-dead gorgeous.

She'd curled her short dark hair into tiny flips that looked like half smiles. Her makeup was expertly applied.

Her suit cost more money than he earned in a month, and her shoes were squared at the toe and high. She wasn't at all the frightened woman he'd encountered last night, but a big-time, highfalutin Atlanta doctor.

"I'm here because I couldn't find my cabin in the dark."

She rolled magnificent gray eyes at him and brushed past. "By the way, you're welcome."

Jake's head snapped back. She smelled of vanilla and musk, a sultry combination designed to allure. He had to stay focused. "I—you . . . What are you doing here?"

She lifted her foot over her clothes and maneuvered her open suitcases until she picked up a matching purse.

What would she need that for? The center was two minutes away.

"Well, *Doctor Einstein,* I'm in your house because that's the second time I've had a run-in with your friendly neighborhood bear. *And* because I didn't want to be eaten alive when your furry friend awoke me this morning, trying to get into my car. *And* because I needed a shower, which, by the way, is out of hot water."

"It's a thirty-gallon tank!" What was she, a whale? "No normal person—" Jake said, trying to ignore her bland expression.

"No normal person," she said, cutting him off, "would send a woman into the woods in the dead of night with black bears roaming around."

"You were being difficult, and I didn't know bears were even around," Jake argued back.

"Or," she continued, "go running without protection from beasts."

"Black bears are plant eaters," he shot back, then realized how stupid he sounded.

"Then he must be a gay bear!"

A beep sounded and Shayla consulted her watch. Her demeanor changed before his eyes.

"It's a quarter till seven. Don't bleed on my clothes."

She gathered an old posterboard from the previous year's blood drive, Jake's hammer, a box of nails, and his rifle.

Jake almost hit the floor. She'd tied a lime-green scarf to both ends to make a strap, and slung it over her shoulder.

"Whoa, whoa, whoa," he stammered. "What about all your stuff?"

"What about it? First, I'm not going anywhere I can't

find, and second, I don't want to be late." She pulled the front door open. "If this is the best hospitality you can offer, you need a refresher course."

Hospitality? What more did she want? She'd taken over his house! "Where are you going with my rifle?"

"To work," she said, her gaze searching for incoming predators.

Jake wanted to ask what she'd been doing in his closet, but she was already on a roll. "And that's another thing," she snapped. "You need to keep your gun cleaned. This thing almost took off my shoulder."

Her Georgia accent dripped attitude and so did her swinging hips as she walked toward the clearing that led to the center.

Jake watched in horror as she snatched a snippet of fabric off a tree and nailed a white board to the tree trunk.

A large red arrow pointed at his house.

Written unevenly in red marker was HOME.

Four

Shayla marched through the woods, terrified. She'd never shot at a living thing before. Sure, she'd fired a gun; it was practically a woman's rite of passage in the Crawford family.

But never at an animal. Never at something breathing.

Her hands shook as she snatched white lace off branches that she'd marked earlier, and hammered nails into the trees, hanging her arrow signs.

Mississippi dirt clung like paint to a canvas on her Prada shoes. They were a mess, all because Jake Parker had wanted to get himself eaten by a bear.

She snatched another piece of lace off a branch and walked on her toes. Maybe they could be cleaned by a store in town. Granted, these shoes weren't as dressy as she normally wore, but this was a clinic.

The patient flow probably wasn't anything like that of her father's booming practice. Shayla figured she'd spend most of the first few days training on the software and reviewing procedures.

She'd have lots of sit-down time. The shoes were fine. They matched her gray silk suit perfectly.

When the bushes rustled, a cry of fear raced up, and Shayla double-timed her steps, but she refused to scream. She wasn't a girly girl. She was a Crawford, made of tough stuff that men admired.

The sound of hammer against nail echoed off the swollen forest, but she continued to retrace her steps.

If only she'd found her cabin this morning instead of seeing Jake running and the bear hot on his trail, she'd have been able to take her shower, get settled in, and be to work on time. But no. She'd had to rush, and without coffee the day would likely be dangerous for someone.

The forest widened and Shayla saw her car, Ms. Blue. On her way over, she saw movement in the dusty building window, and noticed the three half-moon heads that tried to spy on her.

Which one of you left the welcome sign? The one who spoke first.

Shayla swiped at her shoes, threw the hammer and extra signs in the backseat, grabbed her purse and the welcome sign, and strode toward the building.

Gray stairs sagged across black concrete and creaked beneath her feet. At the top, she turned the knob and walked inside.

What she saw turned her stomach.

The waiting room was filled with metal chairs, the kind old churches used when volume rather than comfort was the priority.

There was no magazine rack or brochure shelf against the wall. No fish tank or video games to amuse the children. No footstools for pregnant mothers to rest their feet, and no cheerful receptionist to greet her with a cup of coffee.

This was indeed hell.

None of the ladies offered her a hand over the deliberately wedged chairs, so Shayla hiked up her skirt. A long-ago boyfriend had once said she had legs like a colt's, and from that day, Shayla had never been ashamed to show them. Tall for a woman, she gave the ladies an eyeful as she inched the skirt higher and higher, and gracefully tossed her legs between rows of chairs until she no longer leaned on the door for support.

When she was finally over, she'd managed to preserve her dignity, but little else. The ladies' eyes were wide until the door banged shut. Now it was just her and them.

Shayla kept her mouth clenched shut as she looked past the three women to the drooping floor-to-ceiling shelves, crammed full of *paper* medical charts.

This place was straight out of the Stone Age!

She'd visited offices where there was elementary computer use, but here there wasn't a computer in sight! To her inexperienced eye, there had to be thousands of files against the wall.

Two dingy windows filtered in the sun, aided by a flickering overhead fluorescent light. A dark hole at the end of the room was, she supposed, the bathroom, but her stomach turned at the prospect of finding out.

Dismay and shock made her turn. This couldn't be real. Nobody practiced medicine under these medieval conditions.

She accidentally kicked the leg of a chair, and a startling racket ricocheted around the room. The three women behind the makeshift counter laughed.

"I told you she wouldn't last a day," the largest one

said. "Pay up, Jessie." She spoke to a skinny girl with inquisitive eyes. "I'm gone eat that five dollars for lunch."

"I told you I wasn't betting, Pearline." Jessie's voice was soft compared to her coworker's.

"You owe me five dollars. She isn't staying."

Just who does this woman think she is?

Shayla hated this armpit of hell, but that didn't mean she was going to run off like a coward.

They would have to come up with better than a sign and nasty chairs to make her leave. The way things looked, these clueless blockheads needed her to drag them at least as far as the twentieth century.

Shayla knew the enemies from the allies. "Who is the 'she' you're referring to?"

The woman sucked her teeth and dropped her hand to her big hip. "You," she said boldly. "I know everybody else's name in here."

"Pearline, is it?" Shayla walked around the counter, through a low door, and right up to Ms. Mouth. "I believe this belongs to you." Shayla pushed the welcome sign into her startled hands.

Embarrassment forced Pearline's sparse eyebrows up, but she couldn't back down. Not in front of her friends. She crossed her arms. "So?"

"My name is Doctor Crawford. Not she, her, or you. If that's too hard, you can simply call me Doctor." The woman's chin shifted, but she didn't go off as Shayla expected. "The sooner we establish an understanding, the better, Pearline."

Shayla dismissed Pearline and moved to the forty-something woman on the right who'd busied herself shuffling files. Shayla stuck her hand into the woman's line of sight, and when her hand was grasped, Shayla applied pressure until their eyes met.

"I'm Doctor Crawford. And you are?"

"How do you do, Doctor Crawford," she replied carefully. "I'm Dee, the office manager. If you need anything—" She smiled, but a look from Pearline had her frowning. She released Shayla's hand. "Don't hesitate."

"Thank you, Dee. It's nice to meet you."

Shayla moved down to the tentative soldier that completed the awkward trio. Reed thin under outdated jeans and a stiffly tucked-in T-shirt, the woman looped her hand behind her back and twisted her upper body.

"Jessie, I'm Doctor Crawford."

"Nice to meet you," she said pleasantly. "I'm the assistant nurse. Whatever you need, I'll do it for you. Okay?"

Shayla couldn't express how much she appreciated Jessie's enthusiasm. "Thank you," she said sincerely. "Is there any additional staff?"

Pearline gave Shayla a smug look. "What you see is what you get."

Shayla put her purse on the desk. "I can see you have a problem."

Pearline did the whole neck-rolling thing and looked from Dee to Jessie and back to Shayla. "Ms. Thang, I don't have a problem."

"What did you call me?"

Pearline snatched up the files Dee had been fidgeting with, sidestepped Shayla, and shoved the files into the wall, misfiled.

Another thing to deal with, Shayla noted, but stuck to the situation at hand. These people were going to respect her.

"I asked you a question."

"I heard you the first time, like I know you heard me."

This time Shayla drew back. "Oh, no, no. You will call me Doctor Crawford or—"

"Or what?" she demanded.

"Come on, Pearline. Why do you always start trouble with the new doctors?" Jessie rested her elbows on the counter, her chin in her hands. Braids hung past her shoulders, taking years off her young life. She looked all of fifteen.

Pearline worked up a sweat as she marched into the waiting room and realigned the chairs. "She's the one who came in here with her fancy-schmancy car and silk suit. I don't kiss nobody's butt."

"You're the one with the attitude," Shayla informed her. "If you don't like me, fine. But you will respect me. If that's too much to ask of a staff member, you can leave."

The room stilled and every eye shifted. Beads of sweat dribbled down Pearline's face and she wiped at them angrily. "You can't make me leave."

"You're right. That's your choice. But rules will be obeyed and if anyone has a problem, I'm sure Alberta's unemployment office will welcome you." She stared down Pearline. "Are you here to work or are you leaving?"

Rage tore across the woman's face and she ran out the door.

Seconds later, a car tore out of the parking lot.

"Why did you say that?" Jessie cried, coming around the counter. "She's mean, but she's not a bad person." She ran out the door after the woman.

"That's an oxymoron, if I ever heard one." Shayla looked at Dee. "Is this some kind of initiation?"

Dee shook her head.

Shayla felt as if she were at the bottom of the ninth with no runners on bases. "Where's my office?"

"This way, *Doctor*," Dee emphasized.

Shayla followed Dee down a long hall, with closed doors on either side. There was another tiny bathroom and what she suspected was a supply or coatroom.

Dee stopped at the end of the hallway, flipped a switch on the inside wall, and returned to the front.

The room had been added on at some point, the floor a few inches lower than the main building. Plywood covered these walls, making the room cooler. Pictures drawn by children covered the walls, but the curled edges indicated they were more than a few years old.

Everything was shabby, ragged, or worn. She dropped her purse on one of the two desks that were crammed L-shaped against the wall.

Purgatory took on a new meaning.

Resentment and anger boiled in her and when she turned around, Dee was standing there. "Is there anything you need?"

"Does Doctor Parker prefer a certain desk?"

"Doctor Parker *prefers* to sit up front with us. Will that be all?"

"Yes," Shayla said, afraid if she said more she'd seal her own coffin shut. She pulled tissue out of her purse and wiped off the chair before she dropped into it.

The door to the center slammed against metal chairs, and Shayla's mouth quirked. Muffled voices filtered back, then pounding footsteps.

Shayla looked up into Jake's enraged face. "You better have a very good reason for firing Pearline."

"I didn't fire her, she walked out."

He raised his hand as if to say something, then changed his mind. "Pearline would never *walk out*."

Shayla wasn't up to sparring with him again. She reached for a folder, opened it, and found it full of death certificates. The second least favorite part of her job. She tossed it back onto the desk.

"I could hardly throw her. She stormed out." Shayla rose and leaned against the desk, crossing her legs. "You need better employees, anyway. And where are their uniforms? Nobody would know those three were nurses if they weren't sitting behind the counter."

"I'll tell you what, Doctor Crawford. If Pearline doesn't have a job, neither do you."

"I'm a doctor. Far more valuable than an office assistant." She crossed her arms, daring him to disagree.

A feral look snaked across Jake's face as dread coiled through her.

"Not only do you get your patients today, you'll see Pearline's as well. And by the way, she's a Licensed Practical Nurse."

Shayla couldn't focus on the second statement, her brain stuck on the first. "What do you mean see patients?" she snapped, anger mounting. "I don't even know your computer system, *if* I could find it. I haven't even reviewed your procedures."

Jake grabbed her elbow and guided her into the hallway.

"Here's your training. Exam room one. Exam room two. Supply cabinet and toilet." They ended up at Dee's office. "We don't have a computer system. The medicine is kept here." He pointed to a locked room behind the counter. "The charts are here, and we charge twenty-five dollars a visit. Give each patient a receipt and an appointment for a follow-up as necessary."

He opened the front door and a line of people wrapped around dividers as if they were waiting to get into heaven.

Shayla was stunned.

"These are your patients and Pearline's. At the end

of the day, clean out each exam room, and take out the trash.''

Shayla snatched her arm away, not caring that the one hundred or so patients were watching. ''You're not serious.''

Jake shrugged off his lab coat, and draped it around her shoulders. ''Where do you think you're going?'' she demanded.

''I'm taking the day off to console my sister, Pearline.''

Five

Shayla didn't acknowledge the ache behind her knees from standing in heels, and the lower-back throb that had started somewhere around her sixth hour at the center.

She blocked out the smell of sweaty bodies, and the intense heat in the cement tomb they called exam rooms. She refused to acknowledge anything but work.

She scratched her neck, arms, and throat. But the cracks in her hands hurt worse. There was no such thing as moisturizing soap up here, and she'd washed her hands too many times to count. She hadn't stopped to think about anything except moving patients along, one by one by one.

Most of them didn't believe her when she'd said, "Doctor Parker's taken the day off, that's twenty-five dollars, please." But soon the word spread and the more difficult questions followed.

Who was she? Where was she from? Why was she

dressed up as if she were going to a funeral? How old was she? Was she old enough to be a doctor?

She'd stopped answering by noon. By six that evening, Shayla was barely speaking at all.

Between her father and Jake threatening to put her out, Shayla's self-esteem was close to the breaking point. She stared up at the wall of misfiled charts. "How is anybody supposed to find anything in here?"

"We manage," Dee said.

"Well, that's not good enough." Shayla dumped out a laundry basket of gowns, and scanned the section of files for Grant. She found every misfiled G file and threw them in the basket.

Dee ran over. "What are you doing?"

"Housekeeping." She moved around Dee and called Grant's name.

Hours later, Shayla looked up from her last exam to the door of the exam room. Dee stared down at her.

"I'm leaving now."

"Night." Shayla wanted to thank Dee for sticking out the day, but the words just didn't come.

"Good night."

Shayla's feet ached as she changed the exam table.

Silence broke her automatic pilot state, and she knew the day had ended. She walked to the doorway devoid of whispers, crying babies, and the moans of the sick.

It was time to go home.

Trash bags lined the hallway wall, and Shayla damned Jake again. This was a fine way to repay someone who'd saved his life. Next time she'd throw a raw steak on him to better her odds.

Shayla was halfway out the door when she remembered she was supposed to do something with the money.

She counted quickly and was astonished to know she'd

collected nearly four thousand dollars. Some of the patients had even paid overdue bills. One by one, she opened the desk drawers, searching for a safe or lockbox.

Angry, Shayla stuffed the money in a plastic bag, gathered the garbage, her keys and purse.

Jake would plead for mercy before she finished yanking his hair out one strand at a time.

Gravel crunched under her feet and her ankle twisted. She'd pull out his nose hairs, too. And pluck his eyebrows with her dad's lawnmower.

Shayla reached the closed Dumpster and stared at it. "Are they crazy?"

She looked around for a rock or stick, but it was dark and she was tired. Her eyes burned and she wanted to cry, but she didn't believe she had the energy.

She took a tentative step toward the Dumpster, holding her breath. If she could raise it enough, she could toss the top back and throw in all the bags, but her hands wouldn't follow her brain's order to touch the grimy, dirty lid.

Wrapping her hand in the long end of the plastic bag of money, she lifted the lid and fought a gag as she flicked it. Every time it slammed closed, a rush of stinky air would cloud her face. Shayla wanted to die.

Finally it opened enough, and Shayla tossed in almost all the bags, but three were just out of reach. For the second time that day she hiked up her dress and stretched to get them, when her hand slipped and the money fell inside.

Her stomach pitched.

Something inside the Dumpster scuttled and Shayla ran to her car.

Wildly she yanked on the locked door, but couldn't get in. "Hello," she cried out. Shayla searched for the path to Jake's, but hadn't hammered a sign to the last tree. In the middle of the night, everything looked the same.

A sob jumped out.

Not only was her purse at the back of the building, but so were her keys. She staggered up the stairs of the center, but the door was locked.

She had no choice but to go get her purse and keys.

She stumbled around the back, swatting at mosquitoes and other human-preying bugs, found her belongings, and ran to her car. Tears clouded her eyes, but she made it inside.

Tears seared the rash that covered her neck.

Kicking off her shoes, Shayla lowered the seat, pulled the sweater she'd used as a pillow the night before, and fell asleep.

Jake scaled fresh fish and handed them to his efficient sister, tuning out every two words.

"I don't care who she thinks she is. I'm not going back."

"You shouldn't have put up that sign." Jake looked at his tender palms and remembered the woman who'd taken on a black bear for him.

"She's a stuck-up, snotty, rich doctor from Atlanta. And she's ugly!"

The level of Pearline's hostility toward Dr. Crawford surprised him. Especially since she'd never treated any of the other doctors this way. "Now that's a complete lie. If anything, she's the best-looking doctor we've ever had."

"I should have known you'd think that. Men," she muttered, disgusted. "*Call me Doctor Crawford or Doctor*," she mimicked, sucking her teeth. "I can't stand high-yellow women. They think they're better than everybody else since they ancestors was closer to the big house than ours. You should have seen the way she looked around the center, like it was full of maggots. That Sasquatch had her nose so high in the air, she shoulda been able to sniff all the way to heaven."

Jake's head popped up. "Now that's enough. She might not be what we expected, but she's what we got, and we can use the help. Besides, you know how this place strikes newcomers."

Jake couldn't believe he was defending Dr. Crawford after the way she torpedoed his house. "I can't do twenty-four hours, seven days a week anymore. That's not fair to the patients or me."

Pearline still pouted. Ten years his senior, his sister looked more like their mother every day. She also had their mother's stubborn will. "I'm still there, Jacob Parker, and I don't aim for you to forget that. We might need someone, but not her."

She breaded the fish and lowered it into hot grease. Pearline studied the bubbles as if they held the answer to her troubles. "She's gonna change everything, Jake. Even you."

"Hey," he whispered, turning Pearline toward him. "She can't change me. We've punished her enough. We're going to work tomorrow and you're going to apologize."

Pearline struggled in his arms. "What about her?" she shot back. "Is she going to apologize to me?"

He kissed Pearline's cheek and returned to his fish.

"I don't know. But I expect you to set the example and try to get along with Doctor Crawford, because if she leaves, I don't know that I can keep the center open with just us."

He'd never said these words before. Never threatened to sell out.

"You wouldn't do that," she whispered. "You promised."

"I'm tired, Pearline. I can't give good medical advice if I can't think."

Her expression softened. "I'll try for your sake."

Six

Jake awoke to the smell of brewing coffee. For a moment he was transported back to med school and his girlfriend Taisha who couldn't function without at least ten cups a day.

But as he opened his eyes and took in the surroundings he'd called home for the past eight years, he knew it wasn't Taisha in his kitchen, but one uninvited guest.

Annoyed, Jake dragged a T-shirt over his head. It didn't matter that he didn't lock his doors. Dr. Crawford shouldn't have taken his not saying "get the hell out" as an open-ended invitation to help herself to his life.

He walked into the remnants of Tornado Shayla. Clothes were everywhere, and spike-toed shoes lay like land mines against the solid-wood floor.

"Doctor Crawford?" he called and received no answer. She was gone, just as she'd come.

Jake showered in record time, taking an extra five minutes to iron. He wasn't doing it because Dr. Crawford was so put together, he told himself. His pants had dried too hard over the back porch, and ironing them was a way to soften the material.

He creased them, just because he was standing there.

Jake walked into work at 6:45 A.M. and felt as if a mule had kicked him.

Shayla was sitting in front of the patient charts, her silk jacket forgotten on a metal chair. His first instinct was to straighten it, but he was captured by the way her pretty hands slid across the colored tabs. They glided with precise intent.

When she found the spot she wanted, her left hand wiggled up and held the space while she filed the chart in its rightful home.

Every once in a while, Shayla would dig into a bag of chips and reach blindly for a cup of coffee, but her hands never stopped moving.

"What are you doing?"

She didn't slow down or seem surprised he was behind her.

"Your staff either doesn't know how to read numbers or they're blind. These things are color coded for a reason. Here you are," she said to a file. She yanked it from the wall and dropped it on her lap.

To be beneath her hands. Feeling their soft caress . . . Jake shut the door on his misdirected thoughts. "Why are you doing this?"

"So that when *foreigners* come in here, they can find what they need right away." She might as well have added "moron" to the end of her statement.

Jake walked over and started at the top, running his finger along the jackets. Numerically in order to the point she was working on, the last row. Jake had known their filing system was outdated, but he and Dee hadn't the time to reorganize.

Somehow they'd found files when they needed them. But Shayla was right.

"How are your hands and knees?"

"Scabbing, very little puss." Jake bit his tongue and stared up at the water-stained ceiling. *That was stupid.*

"More than I needed to know," she told him. "But I guess I asked."

"Can I at least help—"

"No!" She grabbed the file from his hands. "If you want to do something, unstick the door to exam room one."

"Fine. I was just offering." He'd spent half the night feeling bad they'd been too rough, but apparently not.

"Oh, like you offered yesterday?" She grabbed a stack of charts that were about knee high and dropped them into the laundry basket. "No thanks, Doctor. I think I can shoot myself in the head all by myself. Where does the night deposit go?"

"In the drawer."

She turned back to him and looked at the desk. "In that thing?"

The desk was old, but it was sturdy. "Yes, why? Where is it?"

"I was taking out the trash, and, well—"

She left the room and Jake resisted the urge to run after her. She came back and beelined for her chips and coffee.

"Where's the money?" he repeated.

"It fell into the Dumpster." She gathered another load of files and walked into room two.

This time he did follow. "What!"

"Why doesn't this room have a chair?"

"Forget the chair," Jake snapped. "I'm still talking about the money."

"Well, I'm not." She faced him, her arms heavy with the files. "Either take these or move."

Everything about her insulted him. He moved as she strode past him and into their office. She dropped the files into his chair and floor. "We need a rug."

"For the floor?" Where was this going?

"No, for the wall. All the walls."

Jake had never seen anyone so unpredictable. "You'd better find a way to get that money."

"You left me here to care for more than one hundred people. No instructions on where things were, or for that matter how to lock up the money. I had to take out the trash," she yelled, poking him with her finger. "And by accident, I dropped the money. If you want me to stay, you go get it, because at this point, I don't think money retrieval ala garbage Dumpster is in my job description!"

Jake felt as if he'd been dropped into a wind tunnel. Shayla wasn't mad, she was steaming, but he wasn't backing down. "I'm not getting anything."

She crossed her arms, her eyes narrowed into slits. The building shook and the files on the chair wiggled with the presence of a large truck. "I think the garbage man is here."

Panicked, Jake ran toward the door. "I'm not finished with you."

"I'll be waiting," she said, still angry.

"Morning, Doctor Crawford. Wow! The files look great," Jessie exclaimed.

Shayla was mad, but she cooled under Dee's sorrowful expression. She still hadn't said a word, but she glided her finger across the files. "I've always wanted to get this done. I guess I can mark it off my list." She sighed and hung up her jacket.

Before Shayla could say anything, a man walked in.

He'd come in the day before looking for Jake, but had accepted her diagnosis of a minor problem. He'd paid his twenty-five dollars and frankly, Shayla hadn't expected to see him again.

Shayla got out her laptop computer and plugged it in.

"Major Spears." She silently congratulated herself for remembering his name. "Is that ingrown toenail still bothering you?"

"No, ma'am!"

Jake walked in, the plastic bag in his hand. "Eeeu-uww," Jessie exclaimed. "Jake, you stink."

"Here," he said to Dee. "Let me wash up and I'll be right up. Jessie, complete the morning opening routine."

He walked into the staff's rest room and slammed the door.

Shayla didn't even blink. She typed in the major's name and the condition she'd treated him for.

No one spoke. Jake walked back in and he and the major shook hands. "How are you today?"

The major glanced at Shayla, then Jake. "I need to see you in private."

"That's just fine. I see you met Doctor Crawford. Had a problem with your foot."

"Yes. Toenail, I'm embarrassed to say. But, uh, she gave me something and it's going to be fine."

"Doctor Crawford, did you know the major served in Vietnam?"

"No, I didn't. I have an uncle who's a career man in the military."

"What branch?"

"Marine Corps."

"Tough guys," he said with respect.

"Affirmative."

The major smiled at the familiar lingo.

Jake talked to the major, and one thing Shayla had to admit, no matter how angry he made her—Jake knew his patients. She typed the detailed and extensive facts about the major's medical history.

"Doctor Crawford, I need to confer privately with Major Spears."

A line of patients formed in front of Jake, but as he moved past Shayla, the line shifted also. Soon fifteen people were against the hallway wall.

Everyone stared at the floor.

Embarrassment heated Shayla's face and she fought the urge to scratch her neck. Behind the last patient, in walked Pearline.

Shayla caught Jake's sleeve. "I saw each and every one of them yesterday."

Dee set the sheet on the counter and waited for instructions.

"Mr. Grimes," Shayla asked, "are you having a problem different from the matter you were seen for yesterday?"

The room was already deathly silent. "I was hoping to see Doc Parker, ma'am."

A look of triumph shot across Pearline's face at the chorus of "me too"s.

Shayla's eyes shifted to Jake. He seemed to be grappling with inner emotions, but she couldn't help him. She'd been one of his biggest problems since she arrived.

"Major, move forty chairs outside."

Jake addressed the patients as a group. "If you haven't been seen in the past week, I'll see those patients first in order of emergency."

A protesting murmur vibrated throughout the room.

"I'm here, Jake," Pearline said, taking authoritative strides across the room.

"You're with me," he told her. The words deflated the bounce in her step, like a pin to a balloon.

The major walked back in.

"All set?" Jake asked.

"Yes, sir."

"Everyone who was seen yesterday and isn't having an emergency, wait in the area outside. If I see you and concur with Doctor Crawford's diagnosis, you'll have to pay the full office visit fee of twenty-five dollars."

Jake looked from Shayla to the wary patients. He'd done as much as he could.

The rest was up to her.

Seven

Shayla picked up her laptop and blinked back her tears, surprised she could do both and keep her head up. Leaving home had been traumatic, but being rejected by the patients was devastating.

Dee verified the previous day's accounts receivables, and gave Jessie the deposit and a list of errands.

Shayla walked into the waiting room and approached the man in the first seat. "May I sit down? Please," she added, knowing if she failed with him, she might as well pack and go home.

"Go 'head."

She perched the laptop on her legs and signed on. The screen took a few seconds, but with each passing second, the more interested other patients became. "What's your name?" she asked.

"Peter Moore. Where you from?" He watched her fingers move across the keys.

"Atlanta. Marital status?"

"Married thirty years. Why you come here all dressed up?"

Shayla glanced up from his chart and cast a blank look at her outfit. This wasn't one of her favorite suits, but it was the first thing she grabbed that hadn't been wrinkled.

"I always wear a suit to work. Age? What should I have worn?"

Mr. Moore shrugged. "Sixty-five. Something like what old Dee has on. Jeans are the best thing for ladies up here. 'Cept on Sunday, of course."

Shayla looked at Dee and definitely wanted them to get uniforms. It helped establish them as professionals. Shayla took his temperature and blood pressure.

A young Mexican woman walked in, two children in tow. She signed the sheet and sat in the last row.

"I don't think I have any jeans," Shayla told Mr. Moore. "What do you do for a living?"

"I refurbish air conditioners. You're in the country," he informed her as she looked at the profile she'd created in her system for him. "You got me in there, right?"

"I sure do," she said when a thought occurred to her. "How much would a used air conditioner cost?"

"Depends on the size. For one of these windows, I'd say about fifty bucks. You learn how to do that in medical school?"

She saved his information. "What? Type?"

"Yeah. You're pretty good at it," he complimented.

She wanted to tell Peter Moore that she'd been in med school for eight years and had graduated at the top of her class, but that would only widen the chasm between them. So she bit her tongue and said, "Thank you."

He patted her shoulder. "You're mighty welcome."

"Come on, Moore," Dee said from the counter. "Doctor Jake is ready to see you."

Shayla handed him a slip of paper with his vitals printed on it. "Take this. It'll help the doctor move along faster."

"You'd be prettier if you said please," he said kindly.

"P-please," she stammered.

"She's a quick learner and a good typer," he said to Dee.

"I think we'll keep her," the manager said and winked at Shayla.

Her spirits soared. Shayla moved on to each patient, and found herself getting other information like where to get groceries and her hair done.

Dee moved around her soundlessly. The waiting room was so quiet and Shayla wondered why there wasn't even a television in the lobby.

She refused to believe everything was about money. Even if they couldn't get more funding, surely they'd sought donations from the private sector.

On the way out, Mr. Moore stopped to thank her and made a five-dollar payment on his account. Shayla noted this.

Jake had told her to collect twenty-five dollars from each patient. Today, they paid only a few dollars.

She reached the Mexican woman with the children who hadn't moved from her side. "May I help you?"

Shayla received a note. *Jessie* was printed on the paper.

"I'm Doctor Crawford. May I help you?"

"No speak English," she said softly, before taking the children's hands. "Doctor Parker?"

"He's with a patient."

Disappointment slid down her face. She spoke to the children, who grasped her hand, and she headed for the door.

"Uno momento!" Shayla called in embarrassing Spanish, ashamed that she'd spent two years in Senora Rita's class.

"Are you sick?"

"No INS," the woman said and started to cry.

"Let her go. There're other people here who are really sick."

"Zip it or you'll be last," Shayla snapped at a man who'd come in yesterday complaining of back pain. He'd demanded muscle relaxers—one hundred of them. Shayla had given him a prescription for ten. He'd left very unhappy. Quieter, she said, "No INS. I'm Doctor Crawford. Dee," Shayla said. "Please hand me my purse."

Dee passed it over the counter.

Sorrow twisted Shayla's heart. She'd seen sick people, but never someone so frightened. She pulled out her wallet and showed the woman her driver's license. "That's me." She pointed. "This is my father. *Mi* papa."

Although the woman hesitated, she looked at Shayla's outstretched hand. *"Sí,"* she said after a quick glance.

Shayla pointed to the little boy. "My little brother."

This time the woman leaned in and giggled softly. "Bad boy."

Her English was tentative, but Shayla got the message and laughed. *"Sí,* Damon is bad."

More confident the woman wouldn't run, Shayla gathered her computer and took it to the counter. "Dee, plug this into the phone jack for me."

"I don't know about that." She looked more than suspiciously at Shayla. Shayla threw caution to her career and pleaded with Dee. "Please? I can help her."

Dee did as she asked, and within seconds she was in a translation Web site. "I'm Doctor Shayla Crawford," she typed and spoke at the same time. "What's your name?"

"Eliza Gonzales. Marc. Dina," she said, giving the children's names.

Shayla typed *Are you sick, Mrs. Gonzales?*

"No, Marc." The woman reached over and typed, *Has a rattling in his chest. Lots of coughing and shortness of breath. Sometimes we can't stop him. He almost passes out.*

Shayla read the message and pulled out her stethoscope. Marc hid behind his mother, but Shayla still reached for him. "You're a big boy. Come here."

"No," he said clearly.

"You speak English?"

"No."

His mother typed, *He says no to everything.*

Shayla dug into her purse and pulled out a brightly wrapped red sucker. Marc reached for it. "No. Dee, type so Eliza can read what I say." She put the sucker in her pocket and looked at Marc. *Not until you let me listen,* Dee typed for her.

He still hesitated, so she compromised. *I'll make you a deal. You can hold the sucker, if you let me listen to your chest.*

Marc considered a moment, then stuck out his hand.

Shayla kneeled down so they were eye level, hooked her stethoscope in her ears, and held out her arms. *Come get it.*

Marc came to Shayla, and everyone applauded.

Night kissed the dark sky with coolness and quiet. The only activity was from the bugs that swam in the headlights of Shayla's car. She leaned her back against the driver door, her feet on the passenger seat.

Tired, she tried to talk herself into finding her cabin

but her bones wouldn't cooperate. They practically begged her to be still, and she obeyed.

Shayla rested her head on the lowered window and let her thoughts drift. Amy was back now from vacation, and at the Mayo Clinic in a nice office. The course of Amy's life had been charted since her birth. The plan was set into motion with her first breath.

Shayla couldn't say the same, yet the two women had become friends and were now colleagues. Well, she wasn't so sure of that anymore.

Amy would never be caught dead in a town like Alberta, Mississippi. Not even with a flat tire. But Shayla had discovered something she hadn't known she possessed.

Compassion. It was such a simple emotion. Like everyone, she was moved by commercials where little starving children were shown rifling through trash, or their ribs prominently pressed against their skin. She'd felt great sympathy for them. But compassion was something altogether different.

Today she'd learned something about herself.

It was time to find her home.

She longed for a bed. A pillow top preferably. King-size with six-hundred-count sheets and two fluffy feather pillows, Downy fresh.

Shayla scratched her itchy neck and caught a whiff of herself. There wasn't anything fresh about her either.

She opened the door and got out of Ms. Blue.

This center wouldn't be half bad, if it wasn't the ugliest, least professional, undervalued place she'd ever seen. It could be something if they fixed it up, and changed their attitudes, and painted.

She dug into a baggie of cereal Eliza had given her. Dinner, she thought, under the starry sky.

Her bladder thrummed. "Shut up."

"Is that how you managed to get yourself sent to hell?"

Jake came out of the shadows, a paper bag in his hand.

"What are you, a spy?"

"Hardly. I love to watch women who sit in their cars talking to themselves. It's a specialty." He approached, the bag extended. "Haven't had dinner, I hope?"

Shayla didn't move. "Why are you trying to feed me?"

"Because despite what you think, Doctor Crawford, I'm on your side."

A delicious aroma wafted over, and her stomach sang a sad melody before she stopped it with a chop to her midsection. *Dogs beg*, she chastised, but excused her mouth for watering.

She swallowed and folded her hands under her arms. "How can you be on my side, when you countermand every decision I make?" Jake slid onto the hood of Ms. Blue. "Hey! Get off my car."

He pulled a sandwich from the bag and sniffed. "Smells like a fried chicken sandwich. You're a good doctor, but you're stubborn."

She didn't care how hungry she was, she wasn't going to be insulted in her home. Rustic as it might be.

"The things you've let go on here are ridiculous," she told Jake without shame. "You don't have half the supplies, staffing, or facilities you need to deal with basic medical situations, and you want to criticize me? Excuse me while I don't listen."

"We can't afford more supplies."

Disbelief struck her. "Why not?"

"We don't have the budget for them."

"Then how are you supposed to help people when we have to ration stupid things like tongue depressors?"

"You come from a place where things are plentiful,

but you'll just have to adjust. We don't have the means to just give things away freely."

"Maybe if you collected money from the patients as you're supposed to, the center wouldn't be broke."

"Easier said than done."

"Then you admit you set me up."

"How's that?"

"You told me to collect a minimum of twenty-five dollars from each patient, and then today everybody is paying pennies on the dollar. No wonder the building is leaning to one side."

"No setup. If you're capable of getting the right amount of money from the patients, then great. Sometimes they have it. Either way, we can't deny them medical care."

Shayla smirked. "I'm glad we agree on that one point because I'm not going to give less just because you're hung up on staying within your budget."

"I have to make sure we have supplies through the winter. We get things when we need them and not a moment sooner."

"You could have gotten more supplies if you'd forecasted differently."

Jake dropped the sandwich back in the bag. "You aren't listening. We aren't eligible for more money. Bottom line."

"Then what about funding from private donors?"

Jake didn't know how to make Shayla understand. He'd lived in this community all his life. The people in positions of power knew of his work, but he got little support from the rich.

Years ago he wanted to open a center closer to Natchez, as some patients were traveling over forty miles to get treatment, but the idea had been shot down. The wealthy in the community had wanted him to extend the practice only so far. "We've done all we can do."

"I think you're limited by your own vision."

"We're doing just fine. Are we clear?"

"No, we're not clear," she yelled, the rash on her neck about as annoying as Jake. Shayla growled in frustration, clawing at her skin.

"Let me have a look."

"No way. I can take care of myself." She forgot her stomach for a moment and scratched. "Something bit me and I can't stop itching."

Jake examined her hands, both sides. "You're frustrated, I know."

His cool compassion touched a nerve in her. "I don't need any of your help, Doctor Stingy."

Jake didn't mind her and tipped her head up.

"Do you have X-ray eyes? It's too dark out here for you to see anything," she snapped, a day's worth of irritation flowing. "You should have motion-detector lights installed out here. But I bet you're too stingy for that too."

He touched her chin, and her stomach zinged. "Agreed."

"That you're stingy?"

"No, Doctor Crawford. That I'll get lights out here. Come on."

Jake guided her up the stairs, Shayla resisting the whole way.

"What are you doing? I'm off for the night."

They walked inside and Jake took her to exam room one. It felt weird being alone in the dark with him. Jake was so quiet and unflustered. Her stomach was doing some kind of funky dance and it had nothing to do with her rash and everything to do with Jake's hands on her.

She turned in his arms. Another step and their

mouths would meet. Shayla had been cursing him all day, and now for some bizarre reason, she wanted to kiss him.

"You're loud. And cranky," he added and patted the table.

"No."

"You want me to examine you in the doorway? Fine, but you might be more comfortable sitting down."

Suddenly her head felt light. Sitting down was a better option than falling down. She slid up onto the table and tried not to scratch. "I am frustrated," she agreed while he waited. "This isn't at all what I expected."

"Every doctor that's come here felt the same." He came toward her, and her stomach started to wiggle again. "You get used to it."

He examined her neck and behind her ears. Shayla breathed in his masculine scent, the hint of something so enticing she leaned in and inhaled.

Jake put his hands on her shoulders. "You okay?"

She immediately straightened. "Just itching."

"You need food of substance. Not just Cheerios and candy."

"Well, I'd eat if I knew where I lived."

"You're kidding, right?"

"No."

He dropped the sandwich on her lap. "Eat."

Shayla removed plastic from one part of the sandwich, the bread and meat combination making her body hum.

Succulent chicken, seasoned and cooked to perfection and smeared with salad dressing, was the most delicious food she'd tasted in her life.

Jake examined her as she chewed. "Your heartbeat is accelerated." He looked into her eyes. "Hungry?"

"Very," she said.

He looked as if he wanted to say more, but didn't.

Instead he pushed up her sleeves to see if the rash had spread.

"What is it?" she asked.

"Be patient."

He looked around her neck and down her collar, moved her arm from in front of her chest. He lifted the flap of her jacket.

"Not itching down there," Shayla said, her mouth full.

"But the rash is there. See?"

She followed the ridge of his finger down the front of her suit to her bra. She stopped his finger just as it grazed the swell of her breast.

"I get the point."

"I'm sure you do. Turn around."

"Doctor Parker," Shayla protested, feeling more embarrassed than ashamed. "I've got a rash. That's it. I'll put cortizone cream on it. I'm fine."

He lifted her jacket from behind, then reached around and undid the last button. "You're fine and contagious," Jake concurred.

"What!"

"You've got poison ivy."

Of course, she thought, looking at the pattern. But she hadn't had access to any for exposure. "Where'd I get that?"

She turned around to his gleaming smile. "Could be the woods, toting a gun, threatening a bear."

"Saving a doctor."

"True." Their gazes held. "Come on. I'll get you fixed up and then you can move into your own place."

Shayla slid off the table. "Why are you being so nice to me?"

"You've had a hard day."

"That's the only reason?" she asked.

"Should there be another?"

Being in such close proximity nearly made Shayla forget they were adversaries. "I deserve the credit for doing a good job. I guess that's too much for you to acknowledge."

Jake gave Shayla a bag with cortizone cream and Benadryl.

He locked up and they walked down the stairs. "The patients are intimidated by you."

"That's a load of hooey."

"You don't like hearing the truth."

Shayla wanted to swear but bit her tongue. "You want to know what's wrong, Jake?"

"No, Shayla, but I'm sure you're going to tell me."

"It's 2002 and your computer system doesn't exist."

"It's broken," he told her.

They slammed into her car and she started it. "The X-ray machine is so old you can hold the screen up to the sun and get a better reading. And the staff is like watching a bad sitcom."

"Leave," he told her.

"You'd like that, wouldn't you? How many doctors have you let run off?"

"People come and go, not because of the staff, but false expectations. You're a spoiled snob, Doctor Crawford, and I use that term loosely."

Shayla slammed on the brake, pitching them against their seat belts. "I graduated at the top of my class. I've worked in gutters that make this place look like Cedars-Sinai. My father and I were in Philadelphia when the World Trade Centers were destroyed. I worked for ten straight days, offering medical care to every person I could. Yes, I'm spoiled. Yes, I'm even a snob, but don't ever imply ever—" She tried to catch her breath. "That I'm not an excellent doctor."

She blinked furiously. "Now get out of my car."

"I'm sorry," he said.

"No—"

"Really, I'm sorry. Come on. Pull over there."

Shayla didn't know what more to say. Her eyes stung, the tears ready to fall. But his apology diffused the hurt just a bit. She eased her foot off the brake and followed his directions. The faster she got there, the faster she'd be rid of him.

"What can I do to make you feel better?" Jake asked.

"Jump in front of my fender and let me run you over."

He chuckled. "No, really. I knew there was a sense of humor in there, right?"

"It's in the Dumpster, with the trash. I want Jessie."

"Fine," he agreed quickly.

Shayla decided to take it a step further. "By the way, I don't do trash."

"Everybody does trash. Including me."

"That's the most ridiculous thing I've ever heard. We're physicians, not waste removal technicians. I don't do trash!"

"If you can't follow the rules, then why don't you go back where you came from, Shayla? This ain't the place for you."

Shayla's insides twisted when he said her name. This was the second time, and she decided to turn the tables on him. "How would you know, Jake?"

He touched the springy tips of her hair.

Shayla remembered the smell of every fight she'd ever had in her life. Anger smelled like hot coals and burning leaves.

But this fight smelled different.

Her nose twitched and she inhaled slowly. Her cheeks warmed and her eyes narrowed. Then it hit her. This was the fight of seduction.

She felt hot, but not furious. Hungry, but not starved.

"What type am I?" she asked him.

"You're a rich—" he said and stopped.

"Say it," she dared him and got the distinct impression he wanted to kiss her. His tongue darted across his lips. His chest puffed up ever so slightly. His hands twitched at his sides. His pulse increased at his temple. His eyes filled with promise and desire.

"Too rich for my blood."

She didn't believe him. "I'm ready to go."

They got out of the car and walked through the woods for a short distance that ended at the front door of her cabin.

"It's not hard to get here." Jake turned on his flashlight and flashed it across the shimmering shallow lake. "That's my place over there."

Across the star-sparkled water was indeed his place. "I never even noticed. How am I supposed to find my way to the center?"

"Easy. There's your sign." He turned the light and pointed about thirty yards north.

Jake walked up the stairs and pushed the door open.

Shayla saw her bags first, neatly lined against the far wall.

"You touched my underwear."

"I didn't enjoy it," he said in the quiet.

She rolled her eyes and followed him. "Thank you—" she said.

A low growl froze Shayla in her shoes.

They turned toward the kitchen. Ravages of an intruder were all over the floor. The refrigerator had been overturned and all the food inside scavenged. It took Shayla's mind just a second to register. Then she hit the door running back the way she'd come.

Eight

"Shayla, wait!"

Jake tore through the woods, afraid the bear would follow him, but more afraid that Shayla would get away. He'd already calmed her down, her bout of poison ivy not the worst thing she'd experience—*if* she stayed.

But if she got hurt, or worse, made it back to her cute little BMW, he was sunk.

The truth was he needed her. Couldn't run the center without her. He'd tested her and she hadn't backed down, but the bear was another story.

Jake stumbled and caught himself on one of her shoes just as her small car bounced onto the dirt road and kicked back dirt.

"Shayla!" Jake stopped running, his breath bursting out. She was gone. And probably wasn't ever coming back.

* * *

Lauren tiptoed out of her daughter's room, her hands tight with worry. She massaged them, wishing she could gather Shayla in her arms the way she used to. She hurried into her bedroom and closed the door. "Eric, what do you think happened?"

He folded back the sheet for his wife. "Baby, I don't know. I tried to reach Jake Parker, but no one answered. The operator said the lines were down from the rain, so I guess we have to get our answers from Shayla once she wakes up."

Lauren slipped out of her robe and gown and climbed into bed next to her husband. He'd always had the power to seduce and calm her with the same touch. Tonight, she needed comfort, yet she didn't find it in his troubled gray eyes.

"She's a grown woman now. We can't baby her," he said, as much for her benefit as his.

Lauren smiled up at the love of her life. Eric tried to act tough, but he was a softy. Shayla was as much his baby as Damon.

Lauren had wondered how love would develop between daughter and father, but they shared the Crawford passion in anger and in love, too.

Eric brought Lauren close. "Mama," he said, trying to ease her worried mind, "she'll be fine. We can't grow up for her."

Lauren guided his hand to her lips and kissed his palm, then held it to her heart. "Honey, she's not fine. She's home less than a week after she left. Obviously something scared her more than you. And she's got a terrible rash. She's running from something, and I don't want you to force her to go back."

"What can I say to convince you she'll be fine?"

"I don't know if words are what I need."

Eric kissed the top of her breast, his palm molding it.

Ten years hadn't decayed their passion, nor the pleasure they shared. Her body still excited him and he had to slow down and savor her essence.

"You're distracting me," she purred in her sweetly melodic voice.

"Let's just see what she has to say for herself." Eric kissed her, striving to hear the mezzo-soprano that always signaled her approaching climax.

Lauren moved her head, straining to hold on to her sanity.

"I mean it, Eric."

He covered her breast with his lips, used his teeth to bring her nipple to a sharp point. She tried to lift his head and stop the seductive assault, but Eric was relentless and when he touched her at the heart of her sex, she exhaled in A minor.

"Eric." She sighed.

"I know, sweetheart." He entered her. "I know."

At midnight, Eric sat in his home office trying to review patient charts for the next day, but his mind was almost six hundred miles away.

How could he have done this to Shayla? He'd finally talked to a woman named Pearline who didn't bother to disguise her dislike for his daughter. In fact, the woman's open hostility alarmed him to no end, especially after she'd declared she hoped Shayla was gone for good.

Eric was never more convinced that he'd thrown his daughter to the devil. Why was his highly educated daughter acting as a sanitation technician? It was his fault she was covered in poison ivy. He'd snuck into her room and applied cream to her neck and hands and felt only anger. Her hands had never been so rough and dry. Eric knew what he had to do. Shayla had to come home.

"Hi, Daddy."

"Sweetheart." His heart pounded as he took in the dark circles under her eyes and the angry rash around her neck.

Shayla sank down onto the blue leather sofa Lauren had chosen to brighten his office, and looked pale against the vibrant color.

"Can I ask you something?"

"Sure. What is it?" He was nearly standing.

"Do you love me?"

Eric's back straightened in slow degrees. What kind of question was that? He couldn't help but take her into his arms. "With everything in me, I love you."

"So I should see the goodness in this soon, right?"

A clamp squeezed Eric's heart and dragged him into a vortex of pain so deep he wanted to catch Shayla like he did Damon when his son seemed hell-bent on slamming his head into a wall.

Eric knew he could stop this madness, but the fact that she'd asked the question demonstrated a change he'd been hoping years for.

Eric stepped out on a limb of trust so thin he didn't know if it could support the words he was about to say. "You will see the goodness," he promised.

Shayla's shoulders straightened, and the unsure look in her eyes disappeared, replaced by trust.

She grabbed the navy robe she'd taken from him on her nineteenth birthday, a shaggy old rag, and tucked it beneath her arm.

This was his baby. His firstborn. His heart thundered. If anything happened to her . . . he'd die. "Shayla." Eric hugged her tight. He kissed her forehead and rocked her in his arms. Fatherhood was so hard.

"Don't start crying, Daddy, or else I'll never get out of here."

"You don't have . . ." he started, ". . . go so soon, do you?"

"I need supplies. Do you mind if I raid the cabinets at the center?"

"Not at all." He looked into her eyes. They were already a million miles away or already back in Alberta, Mississippi. She clutched her keys in her hand, the Snoopy key chain still holding everything together. A fraction of light shot through his stormy fears. "I'll go with you," he said. He draped his arm around her shoulder as they headed for the front door. "Did you see your mother?"

"I'll catch her next time."

Eric wanted to use the reel she'd placed in his hands. But she'd have to swim in for this one herself. "I'll give Mom and Damon your love."

He expected an outburst, but she tucked the robe into a rolling duffel bag and grabbed several grocery bags.

"What's all this?" he asked.

"You had lobster yesterday. I didn't. I took the left-overs." She walked out the door. Eric bent, and Shayla's head popped around the door. "Dad," she said impatiently, "grab the rest of the bags. I don't want my food to spoil."

Remnants of his real daughter shone through.

Eric returned home at four o'clock in the morning and set the house alarm. He needed a moment to compose himself. As he stood in the shimmering darkness, their blessings and wealth reflected around him, Eric faced an abiding truth.

He was a complete and utter fraud.

He sank onto the stairs and put his head in his hands. He wasn't a real father. He'd been playing at being a daddy for eight years. Now there were two children, and he was no better at it today than the day he had started.

Over the years, he'd been trying so hard to do the right thing, using instinct rather than practical experience. Only, that's what he'd hoped for eight years ago. He'd wanted to learn how to be a father so that Shayla would have no regrets when she hit womanhood, but it had been a gamble.

He'd cast the dice on this one and was almost one hundred percent sure he was wrong. And even when he'd known he was wrong, he let Shayla return to Mississippi.

He rose from the bottom of the stairs and heard the squeak of his son's rocker. Lauren was up.

What would he say?

Nothing. This situation would play itself out. He slid into the baby-blue room, with the moon casting a white glow over the woman and son he treasured.

"She's gone?" Lauren asked, as she rocked their son, her eyes closed.

"Yes."

His wife reached for his hand and he kneeled beside her, buried his face in her neck, and inhaled.

"You're a very good father."

Eric didn't think so, but Lauren continued to hum the song she'd given him, as he borrowed a bit of her peace of mind.

Nine

Shayla walked out of room two, marigold nectar paint dotting her skin. She left the door ajar and gave the room a nod of approval, especially the four-foot-tall crotchety nurse with the crooked eyes. Tomorrow, she'd add adhesive and Velcro stickers where the children could give the nurse shots. They'd love it.

Shayla made herself go into the office she and Jake shared and turned in a slow 360-degree turn. What color would show her sense of humor? Prove that her ability to laugh was as good as anyone else's?

Bright green walls with a band of whimsical ivy at seat level should do the trick. Shayla painted in broad strokes, her eyes widening with each rollerful against the wall. When she was done, she stood back.

This certainly proved *something*. Jake would get her point.

Shayla stowed the supplies in the trunk and looked toward her cabin. Had the bear moved in?

Although she thought it was ridiculous, she ricocheted her gaze to the black case that held her 9MM Glock, and felt a bit unsure. If she could fire a rifle, she could surely use the gun Aunt Jade had given her as a birthday present.

Cracking her tired back, Shayla began the tedious task of making trips to and from the car, installing items she'd brought from home.

On the second trip inside, new motion-detector lights flicked on. *Ooooh, interesting.* So Jake had listened.

But like a match to dry kindle, the changes she made would certainly set off fireworks.

Tough.

Shayla climbed the stairs, lugging a portable TV/ VCR combo. Tired, she pushed herself, testing her own endurance as this group of practitioners had her patience. She felt like a marathoner who'd hit the point in the race when she could fall down and quit, or turn the corner and start the uphill climb.

She trudged up the stairs with a box and enjoyed a moment of rest as she unwrapped brand-new Disney tapes. At least the patients would be entertained while they waited.

Next she laid out colorful uniform tops the Atlanta staff liked the most, then dragged in the old desktop computer she'd built her patient database program on. Her father was having her office renovated, and Shayla had been glad to feel his support. He fully expected her to return home, and by the time she got there, everything would be ready.

Shayla locked the door to the center, weary but determined. She'd have to hear about her new office at the end of her term here. Leaving home this last time hurt too much.

She slipped behind the wheel and followed the dirt

road to the back of her cabin. Cautiously, Shayla searched the landscape and didn't see any signs of danger. She hit the trunk release, the 9MM in her hand in seconds.

She was ready to take on anything.

On Monday, Jake exited the clearing and stopped short. Shayla's BMW was parked in its old spot. Had she come back just to return her keys and pack her clothes, or was she back to work?

Not likely, after the conversation Pearline recounted with Shayla's father. Dr. Crawford had made it abundantly clear that Shayla's life was in Jake's hands, and if anything untoward happened to his daughter, Jake would be held personally responsible.

The way Pearline had conveyed the message, Jake didn't doubt him for one minute.

After all, there'd been a bear in her cabin.

Why would a rich, well-bred princess who didn't need the money or the aggravation come back?

Jake walked inside, and the scent of fresh paint greeted him. Then he saw his sister's furious face. She held up a shirt. "I'm not wearing this, and that's final."

The colorful top landed on the chair and she started shoving files into the uniformed wall, her every movement making her feelings known. This medical center belonged to her, and Shayla wasn't welcome.

Dee stared at a computer on her desk, while Jessie fingered her new shirt the way a mother stroked the cheek of a newborn baby.

Jake's gaze moved to Shayla. She looked better than ever. She'd bucked the casual dress code, wearing a tailored charcoal-gray suit under a crisp white lab coat and matching gray sandals. She'd done something with her hair, the springy curls complementing her face, just like the intricate gold loops that shimmered from her ears.

She was in a dimension of her own.

"Doctor, Doctor."

Jake realized his mistake. The words sounded too seductive.

His staff stared at him. Jake cleared his throat. "Good to have you back."

"Thank you."

"We've got a full day ahead." Pearline made the unwarranted announcement much to Dee's chagrin. "Jake, I've set up room one because *she's* made room two unavailable to the rest of us."

Shayla walked right up to Pearline. "Pearline, don't ever refer to me as 'she' again. My name is Doctor Crawford. This is a place of business and like it or not, I'm your superior. I don't expect to have this conversation with you again. Doctor Parker promised me room two, now let's move on."

"Jake, is that true?"

"Yes."

"You didn't bother to tell me."

"You're right." The words hung between them. "Something needs to be clear. Doctor Crawford will be working here full-time for the next eleven and a half months. She's entitled to our support and cooperation. Anyone"—he looked at all three ladies—"who has a problem with that needs to get over it."

"I lived forty-three years without anybody dressing me. I'm not wearing any clothes but my own."

"Pearline, you're out of line."

"I didn't come over and dress you this morning, Jake. I didn't expect to come in here and be told what to wear. Cooperation is a two-way street."

Discomfort riddled Jake. How long had his sister been railroading the staff, and him? Was she the reason no other doctor had stayed?

"Dee, Jessie, do you have any problems with the tops Doctor Crawford was nice enough to bring for you?"

"I like mine," Jessie said, giving Shayla a smile of support. Shayla winked at Jessie, but returned cool eyes to Jake.

"I like the top," Dee said hesitantly, "but I wish you'd have asked me. But I'll be glad to wear it."

"It's your choice, ladies," Shayla said.

"Thank you," Jessie and Dee chimed.

"Doctor Crawford, it seems you have two converts." Jake started toward the exam room to see what Pearline's other comment was about.

"What about the TV?" Pearline demanded.

Car doors slammed and Jake heard the chatter of patients.

"I've sat in this lobby for a week and it's boring," Shayla stated coolly. "I thought a little entertainment wouldn't hurt. These are G-rated movies. Nothing that will unduly influence anyone."

Jake saw the shiny black TV/VCR combination and the extensive selection of movies. He'd never thought of bringing a TV to work. He'd always been so focused on meeting the needs of the center, he'd forgotten one aspect of caring for his patients.

Actually caring for them.

Shayla's presence was changing them in ways he never imagined. He and his sister were adversarial and the staff divided.

Yet he had to admit, although unconventional, Dr. Crawford was the breath of fresh air they needed.

"You have an objection to a TV?" Jake asked his sister.

"No." She pouted. "We just never had one."

He threw up his hands. "Fine, now we do. Doctor Crawford, I'd like to see you in the office."

"Why don't we make it room two?" Shayla gave Pearline every reason to close her open mouth. "You'll want to make a comment on that too, I'm sure."

"Have the opening procedures been completed?" Jake barked, wanting to escape the stifling room.

"All done, Doctor." Jessie followed them into the hallway.

"Uh, Jessie, give us a few minutes?" He didn't know how many times he had thanked God for Jessie's easy demeanor.

"Sure. I'll get everything ready for the vaccinations, if that's all right with you, Doctor Crawford?"

Dee froze, the rustling of her lunch bag quieted. Pearline had her hand on the front door, but turned to look at the doctors. Only Jessie, wide-eyed and innocent, awaited Shayla's response.

Shayla gave Jessie's shoulder a pat. "That's just fine, Jessie, thank you." She walked into room two and closed the door.

Dee snatched Jessie into the office, leaving Jake and Pearline alone. "I told you she would change us," she said, her face sad. Pearline noticed his pressed shirt and pants and his recent haircut.

"For the better," he said.

"You say. I don't believe it. What if I can't?"

"You know where I stand. Do what's in your heart."

She gave a curt nod and opened the door.

Jake walked into room two and his back slammed against the door. "When—how—who did this?"

"I did. Go ahead, Doc. Give me your best shot."

She sat on a rolling stool, her long legs drawn together. The sandals caused her neatly manicured toes to perch at the top of her shoe. Jake fought a surge of desire that shot through him. "Are you intentionally trying to piss them off?"

"Pearline doesn't qualify as a them. I'm a doctor. She's a nurse. What don't you two understand?"

"Things would have gone better if you'd asked their opinion or mine. They feel inferior—"

"The only people who would feel inferior about paint from Wal-Mart are close-minded, backward yahoos! Dee liked my room, so did Jessie. What about you?"

"So I'm a yahoo?"

"If the room fits—" she snapped back. "Excuse me, I have a job to do."

"We're not finished here. You could have made everyone aware of your plans so if they had an opinion, they could have voiced it."

"You've worked here forever, and so has your staff. Your opinion *has* been expressed." She got real close to him. "If something as inconsequential as paint threatens you, you'll never be receptive to changes in medicine or technology."

Jake felt as if he'd been slapped. "Look, Shayla—"

"While I'm in this building, my name is Doctor Crawford, and yours is Doctor Parker."

"Fine, Doctor Crawford. You should have asked—" He backpedaled at her slit-eyed glare. "Consulted me."

"No."

The single word decimated his attempt to smooth out the situation. "I'm in charge of this facility. Before you change another thing, it goes by me first. Period."

A beam of sunlight slithered through a crack in the wall and bounced off Shayla's gold bracelets.

He turned to go, then changed his mind and faced her. "You come in here with your five-hundred-dollar suits and think you can run over us little country folks. *You* insult my staff by bringing them clothes they didn't ask for, and *you* shame them by restructuring their work-place without their input."

"Insulting your staff was never my intention, but you act as if there isn't room for improvement. Your office is ill run," she drilled. "Patients' lives depend on the accuracy of those files and the information within them. You should be grateful I cared enough—"

"Grateful? We've been managing just fine."

"Until somebody dies," she ground out. "Then you'd have the state board going over this place with a fine-tooth comb. After they found the one hundred ten violations they could spot from the parking lot, they'd shut down this . . . this hut," she spat, "and revoke your license."

"This center has survived audits, floods, and wars. We'll be here long after you're gone."

She sidestepped him and marched out the door.

"Fine," he shouted and kicked the door closed. "Leave!" Jake dropped his head and cringed.

The door crashed open behind him. "I'm not that easily put off. Especially when I'm right." She slammed six file folders with six different numbers and six different names onto the exam table. He recognized the patient, Major Clive Spears.

She didn't wait for him to look, but opened each jacket and tracked the major's medical history. "Explain why there are six files for Major Clive Spears and why nobody caught that he was prescribed an antidepressant and the allergy drug Hismanal."

Disbelief shook Jake. "The combination could cause heart arrhythmias."

"Major Spears was seen in March of this year with the symptoms scratchy throat, watery eyes, sneezing."

"Allergies."

"The attending physician, Doctor Waycross, prescribed Hismanal. The patient used the Hismanal for a time, then stopped taking it."

"His body had probably adjusted," Jake added.

"A week ago, Major Spears was seen and his complaints were of abnormal agitation, insomnia, headache, and nausea. You switched him from the antidepressant Bupropion to Nefazodone."

Jake studied the conflicting information and his signature on three of the jackets as the last attending physician. Two of the jackets were marked *File Not Found*, indicating the need to have a new file made. He'd never seen the others by the past physicians.

Shayla went on. "A day ago, the patient was seen complaining of an irregular heartbeat."

"I never saw this file." Jake covered his eyes. How could that have gotten by him? He prided himself on knowing what was going on in his patients' lives, but this could have turned fatal.

Shayla lowered her voice, too. "Instead of arguing with me, you should be spearheading any initiative to bring this center into the twenty-first century."

"I agree."

"But what, Doctor Parker?" she demanded.

"Things won't change overnight. Give us the opportunity to work with you on approved changes."

One of her eyes jumped. "Approved changes? Name an approved change." She folded her arms over her chest.

"The painting—"

"Didn't approve."

"TV was a great idea."

She shook her head. "Didn't approve."

"The curtains in the office."

"Didn't approve. Can't, can you?"

"Doctor Crawford, you insult the staff when you do things without consulting them."

"Doctor Parker, it's you who insults your staff's intelligence every time you say 'we can't.' "

"We have a strict budget to maintain. The files notwithstanding, the rest of the things you've done are all window dressing."

"Ever think that's why the medication second to high-blood-pressure meds is antidepressants? This place would make you take a bottle a day, if that were possible. I dare you to make one change."

Jake watched her lined lips, the tint of peach lipstick beckoning him. The lure of her perfume and the challenge in her eyes.

"I don't answer to you. Defy me again, and I'll bounce your butt back to Atlanta so fast your head will spin."

Jake opened the door, but not before he heard Shayla's final words.

"Don't worry about my butt. It's my brain you'd better watch out for."

Ten

Shayla stood on the kitchen chair, the broom in one hand, Raid for wasps and hornets in the other. Something small had scampered across the floor a minute ago, but she wasn't sure if it had run behind the refrigerator or the stove.

It helped that the can advertised a projectile of twenty-two feet, but it didn't help that she was targeting the wrong species.

Her best hope was to drown the four-legged rodent, or slow it down enough to bludgeon it with the broom.

Out of the corner of her eye, gray matter moved and she hit the nozzle, spraying as she screamed.

"Doctor Crawford," a little voice called from outside. "Are you all right?"

Fumes from the outdoor-use-only spray watered her eyes as she inspected the floor around the cabinets. Nothing. Dang. Only a wet spot on the wall the size of a basketball.

Coughing, Shayla opened the door. "Hi, Jessie."

Jessie waved her hand under her nose. "Are you trying to kill yourself?"

"Funny."

Jessie followed her inside and closed the door.

"Leave it open. We need air."

"Well, okay," Jessie said reluctantly. "But a skunk might wander in." The woman settled on the couch, crossing her legs, then wrapping her foot around her ankle.

Shayla slammed the door closed. "You're so skinny. You need to eat more."

"I eat plenty." She picked up the magazine Shayla had been reading. *"Psychology Today?"* She flipped the pages. " 'Why baby boomers' grandchildren can't support themselves.' That's an easy one. Baby boomers made their children work so hard, they in turn gave their children all the things they felt they'd been deprived of, and unwittingly made it impossible for their children to be self-reliant adults."

Shayla wanted to gag. She'd been reading the article for an hour and hadn't seen that at all. Jessie couldn't have been more right.

Bored, Jessie tossed the magazine aside and leaned back. "So, what you doing today?"

Feeling sorry for myself. "I was—ah, thinking of asking the staff if they might like me to get a subscription to the magazine."

"You're so thoughtful," Jessie said sweetly. "But I don't think so. Some people might think you're making a statement, you know, on the slide."

Shayla made a mental note. *Kill rodent with magazine and dispose of both.* "So what brings you by?"

"I figured you needed some company. We missed

you at church and you haven't gotten your hair or nails done.''

Shayla sat in a kitchen chair, gnawing on a hangnail.

"The drug store has clippers, you know.''

"I've got clippers, too. They're called teeth.'' Shayla yanked her thumb from her mouth. "So, what does one do on a Saturday?''

"I don't know about one, but everybody washes clothes, grocery shops, and prepares for Sunday dinner. Then we get our hair and nails done. Sometimes the ladies at church get together and have a ladies afternoon. We go to the movies or to a play. Say, have you been to the Wal-Mart?''

Shayla had lied when she'd said the paint used in the exam room was from Wal-Mart. It was really Ralph Lauren, but then Jake would have been right, and he would have missed her point. She hadn't been in a Wal-Mart in about four years.

"I didn't know there was one close by,'' she lied. "What's going on up there?''

"Today, all the men that work construction over in Biloxi are hanging out at the pool hall down the street from the Wal-Mart. I sometimes stop down with Pearline. Dee claims watching men play pool got her knocked up with both her kids.''

A chuckle rose in Shayla. "Well, I don't think I need anything from Wal-Mart or the pool hall today, but I would like to see about getting my hair done.''

"Your nails, too?''

How could Shayla turn down such a hopeful smile? "Sure. Why not?'' She grabbed her keys and they crossed the unpaved path to her car. Once on the road, Shayla felt immeasurably better.

The sky was painted azure and the sun warmed her face. She was making friends, and she was away from her cabin. Over the past week, she'd walked along the lake, to and from work, numerous times, familiarizing herself with the land surrounding her home. She'd even gone into town Thursday night, but she didn't know everything closed at nine.

"Doctor Crawford?"

"Yes?"

"We should probably stop at the Wal-Mart anyway."

"Why?"

"Because you have more than one mouse. I think a family of mice has moved in with you."

Rain sprinkled Shayla's windshield as she searched out hotels.

Shayla walked into her cabin, her hair freshly done, her nails shiny, her disposition exponentially better than when she'd left, and a smile on her face.

Four bags from Wal-Mart filled her arms as she carefully let the plastic slide to the floor.

Jessie had been an excellent tour guide of the tiny community, taking Shayla places she wouldn't have found if they'd been in the middle of the road.

After shopping and getting their hair and nails done, they'd stopped by Jessie's church where the rehearsing senior choir didn't need microphones, and the floors were made of wood.

The cushioned red pews were close together and comfortable, and Shayla slid back in time to her grandmother's church as the choir sang hymnals of struggle.

Pastor Williamson entered through a back door and pretended to scare Jessie. The two hugged and she introduced Shayla.

The older man sized her up. "Doctor Crawford, are you saved?"

There were many things in Shayla's life she was unsure of, but this wasn't one of them. "Yes, sir."

He patted her hand and walked off in search of another wayward soul.

The pastor's wife, Odessa, was a charming woman who smelled of pressed powder and velvet. She'd grilled Shayla about her family and when she was finally satisfied, invited her and Jessie over the next day for Sunday dinner.

Shayla sat at her kitchen table and rummaged through the bags.

Today had been a good day. Dinner out sounded wonderful. Too bad she hadn't made any friends besides Jessie.

Dee was polite, but she was Pearline's friend. And Pearline would rather see Shayla in the lake than speak to her.

Jake was polite. To a fault.

Shayla acknowledged something she hadn't wanted to since she returned. Jake was someone she liked keeping off balance. That was nothing new, only an unexpected attraction had shocked her yesterday. She'd been angry, but still she'd wanted to back him against the door of room two and kiss the hell out of him.

Between the bear and Jake's attitude, Shayla needed a treat. She popped open a bag of Cheetos and watched *The Terminator,* her favorite movie, for the eighty-fifth time.

Jessie called Mr. Amos and left him in the examination room.

"The patient is in the room, Doctor."

"Thanks, Jessie."

Shayla reviewed his chart before walking in. "Hi, I'm Doctor Crawford. What seems to be the problem?"

"I can't go to the bathroom."

Shayla wanted to die. Was this enema man? She glanced at his chart again and knew before she looked up that he was the dreaded gasbag from the lobby. She took a deep breath and pressed on.

"When was the last time you had a bowel movement?"

"A week ago."

A gas ball shot out and he sighed. Shayla schooled her expression and opened the door. She took a deep breath before turning back to him. "Nothing since last week?"

"Nothing but gas."

"Great. I've got just the thing for you."

He began unbuckling his belt and Shayla stopped him. "No, sir, no enema here. Uh, our toilets can't handle—uh." Shayla coughed, the fumes too much. "They're broken."

"I was looking forward to being out of the house for a while."

"Sorry, but you've got to go."

He looked at her.

"Up front." Shayla kept a bright smile on her face and ushered him out of the room. *The smell is going to corrode my teeth.*

Pearline could barely contain herself. Shayla unlocked the medicine cabinet and withdrew a bottle. "Take two teaspoons and don't leave home afterward. If you don't have any results, come back tomorrow."

"Thanks, Doc. See you tomorrow."

Jessie's eyes watered as he pooted before leaving. She started fanning the door as patients groaned. "Doctor Crawford, he won't get off that toilet for two days."

Pearline's exasperated sigh pleased Shayla. "Are we still going to do the vaccinations?"

"You bet. I'll get our gear."

"The trash, Doctor Crawford. Today is your day," Pearline said.

Shayla gripped the bags without a word and walked outside.

The idea of leaving the center for a day relieved her tension. Pearline might have thought she was intimidating Shayla, but she was sure the woman hadn't ever experienced the trauma of a national tragedy.

While the work here was challenging, it lacked the primitive undercurrent that thrived in a Grady or New York University hospital.

Security at the urban hospitals wasn't rent-a-cops but real police officers who gauged the safety of all by every person who came through the automatic doors.

Doctors shared a unique brotherhood that carried over into their personal lives. But here she was rank and file. A garbage lady in drag.

Jake hadn't been supportive past his speech last week. He hadn't shown any enthusiasm for her effort to professionalize the staff. Her brain tripped over the word, wondering if it were real, too disgusted to care.

The bottom line was, she was trying to help *him* out, and his nonsupportive, misguided dislike of anything that wasn't cheap or poor was about as bad as kicking a door with a broken foot.

She tossed the bag in her hand into the Dumpster and realized that Pearline had thrown away the shirt she'd given them.

They could burn them for all Shayla cared, but she wouldn't be treated like a redheaded stepchild for the duration of her stay in Alberta.

Shayla took a deep cleansing breath and exhaled.

What had happened on the second night she and Jake had stood up to each other on the lot? Had the attraction she'd felt been real or misplaced?

Nothing seemed to be the way it was supposed to be. Back around the building, Shayla lifted the trunk of her car, and gathered the paint cans and brushes.

She didn't need them anymore. Why improve something nobody cared about? She tossed them into the Dumpster and walked back to the front of the building.

Her watch read nine o'clock. "Jessie? Come on. We've got to get going."

Jake stepped onto the porch. "I was looking for you."

"Why?"

"Why haven't you changed?"

Shayla looked at her clothes. "Because I'm wearing this today. Why?"

He was neatly pressed all the way to his golf shirt. "You're dressed all wrong for the work we've got to do."

"We? I thought Jessie and I were going."

"Change of plans." The statement was so simple, Shayla didn't respond. Pearline gave him a helmet and walked past Shayla, followed by a line of patients.

"Why do you need a helmet to drive in my car?"

"Because, Doctor Crawford, you're not taking your car."

"Here are the supplies." Pearline handed everything to Jake. "The ATV's already gassed up. How far do you expect you'll go today?"

"Wait a minute," Shayla said to them. "What the hell is an ATV?"

Pearline gloated. "Oh, you haven't met Rex. It's your transportation for the day. One more thing." She grabbed medical forms from Dee and gave them to Jake.

Pearline pointed to Shayla's legs. "A word to the wise,

cover those legs, or you might get more than you bargain for."

"What's going on here? Doctor Parker?"

"You and I will be working together today. One day a month, we only do blood pressure screenings and other noncritical care at the center so I can go into the community and help people who wouldn't normally come to us. That's today. You are changing, aren't you?"

"No," Shayla said defiantly, feeling as if she'd been set up for the second time in one day. "Let's go."

Jake turned to a very scared-looking Jessie. "Bring me an Epenefrin pen."

"But, Jake—" she whispered.

"We're going to be fine." He descended the stairs, and pushed a radio into Shayla's hand. "You're in charge of communication with base—that's here. Pearline will have the radio on at all times."

Shayla stared at the instrument. "This isn't a cell phone."

Jake shook his head and called on the Lord.

A low rumbling started behind the building, and Jessie appeared straddling an all-terrain vehicle. *ATV.* Shayla cussed under her breath.

Jessie stored the bags in a small covered trailer, then swung gracefully off. Of course she was wearing jeans with dark blue sneakers and the nurse's shirt Shayla had given her.

The black seat was high and wide and Shayla would have to hike her skirt up just to swing her long legs over. Damn them for not telling her, but she wouldn't change now. "Are we leaving now?" Shayla wanted to know.

"Yes, ma'am."

"Fine. I'm ready." Slowly, Shayla inched up the skirt and swung her right leg. She refused to look up to see who witnessed her flagrant display, aware only of Jake's assessing eyes on her standing leg. She didn't make it and had to hike up her skirt a little more. "Doctor Parker?" she said.

"Yes?" His voice sounded as if he were being choked. *Probably on laughter.*

"Come here, please."

Jake walked over, and Shayla used his shoulder as a perch, hiked her skirt to an indecent level, swung her leg over, and settled on the ATV. She steadied her feet and gave the front of her skirt a good yank.

Jake cleared his throat when she looked at him. "My helmet, please."

She shoved it harder than necessary onto her head, jarring her teeth, but didn't say a word. Jessie hooked the radio to Shayla's waist and again offered to go in her place.

Jake wouldn't hear of it.

Shayla wouldn't either. She was going to show Jake Parker and his smug sister that they couldn't defeat her. Jake climbed on and they lurched away.

Eleven

Forty minutes was all Shayla could stand on the back of the ATV. "Please stop."

Immediately, Jake pulled over.

She barely made it to a tree before her stomach emptied.

Jake peeled off her helmet and coaxed her to her knees.

He left her alone for a moment, as Shayla indulged her misery. *This is where I'll die. My forehead embedded in tree bark, dehydrated, tidbits of breakfast dried to the knees of my stockings.*

She wanted to cry, but her stomach rolled again.

The sun beat down in a relentless beam, burning into her pity party. This was her father's fault, she thought, but backpedaled with guilt heavy on her shoulders.

Shayla wanted to blame him, but she'd been immature for too long. This was her wake-up call.

She closed her eyes, and tuned out the noisy birds overhead.

Probably laughing at the stupid human that didn't have sense enough to eat right or wear the proper clothes for a ride through the wilderness.

"Come on, get up." Jake urged her to a shaded tree, where she lay flat on her back, his jacket on the ground beneath her head.

"Tell me this is punishment for a terrible sin I've committed. When will this purgatory end?"

"Purgatory? Isn't that a little overdramatic?"

Ants bit her ankles and Shayla knocked them off. Angry red dots sprang up. "I've never vomited in the woods, in front of a man, in a skirt before! So excuse me for being overdramatic!"

She fell back when her stomach cramped. Jake bathed her neck with a baby wipe. "This is so unlike me," she moaned. "I'm not a helpless female who needs a man to rescue her. I'm independent. A doctor. This isn't my life."

"Here."

Shayla opened her eyes enough to take the wipe he offered. She pressed it to her face.

"Take these."

She took the antacids and her stomach settled a bit. "Thanks."

"This probably is a bit unusual, even for you. But you still have a fine life."

"How can you say that?" she moaned. "Look at me, I'm a mess."

Jake didn't immediately comment. Even though her face was a pale green, with her skirt too high on her thighs, and her jacket gaping enough for him to see the healthy swell of her breasts, she hardly looked a mess.

Jake massaged her tight shoulders. "People would kill to have your life."

Shayla's stomach threatened to mutiny, and she dragged Jake's hand over it and pressed. She breathed in and out. "I don't mean to sound ungrateful. I just—"

"This place can shock the best of them, believe me." Jake saw the thick forest that had been his childhood playground. Through her eyes, she was lost. "It's a good home once you get used to it."

"Did you ever want to leave, Jake?" Homesickness rang in her voice as loud as cathedral bells.

He rubbed her stomach and tried to keep his thoughts professional. "I used to. A long time ago."

"What would have made you leave?"

"I don't know. The right job, money, woman. But not anymore."

Shayla sighed, their gazes locked on the same view, seeing different things. "It's pretty, but I just can't imagine being here forever." The word sounded like a closing steel door.

"Can you make it?" he asked.

Shayla staggered up and steadied herself. "I'll make it." She smoothed down her skirt. "Oh," she cried. "Look at that." A long moan seeped out as she examined her legs. "I can't wear these."

Was she aware that with her long legs slanted out, her hip jutted in the opposite direction and her hands on her thigh, she was at her sexiest?

Jake used to wonder how models struck such odd poses and were considered sexy. Now he knew.

"How much farther?" Shayla asked, unaware of his train of thought.

"Ten minutes. Give or take a few."

"Turn around."

"Beg your pardon?"

"I can't wear hose with runs in them."

She'd just vomited all over a tree. Laughter shot out of him before he could stop it.

"What's so funny?"

"You were just sick as a dog, but now you're worried about runs in your stockings. Seem a little strange to you?"

She rolled her incredible gray eyes. "Can you just turn around?"

Jake didn't even bother. He went to the ATV and got on.

But he heard the whisper of leaves beneath her feet as she pulled the hose from her legs. And her sigh of success once she'd yanked them free of her feet. Hearing her undress was probably worse than seeing her. His mind filled in the blanks extensively.

"I need a mint." Shayla stood next to him, her mouth covered with one hand and the other filled with silk stockings.

He tore into the trailer and gave her mints, then stored the hose as she got on.

Jake was proud of his self-control. He made the ten-minute drive in seven minutes, and had hit enough bumps on the way that Shayla's breasts didn't have time to leave indelible marks in his back.

Shayla climbed off first. She dug through the bag and popped more mints into her mouth. She offered one to him and Jake took the candy. She got in his face. "Do I smell?"

Was she crazy? Jake touched her waist with the intention of moving back, but he found himself bending toward her, close enough to kiss her. Their eyes met. "No, you don't."

Shayla moved first and turned, her attention on the view of Mississippi's impoverished.

The hundred-year-old structure had once housed a wealthy family, the original landowners dating back to the early 1800s. But jobs had moved families closer to the river, and many homes such as this had been deserted.

Now migrant workers, mostly Cuban or Mexican, occupied the houses, although many black families had remained in the area.

Weathered gray wood planked the walls, the paint peeled back like skin off a knee. Poverty was evident by the swirling dust around the porch where azaleas used to bloom and in the clack of a loose shutter. Windows shined, despite the taped panes.

The only thing that remained the same was the clothesline, hanging the weekly laundry.

In the distance dogs charged, their barks loud and menacing.

"Doctor Crawford, don't move. Don't move."

Five Dobermans surrounded them.

"Who is it?" a distinctly Spanish voice said.

"Doctor Jake Parker. May I come in?"

"H'lo, Senor Jake. Is lady from INS witchu?"

"No. She's the new doctor. This is Doctor Crawford."

"You not lying," the voice said.

Jake shook his head.

Shayla stood riveted in place. "Hello," she called. "I'm Doctor Crawford. I'm friends with Eliza. I know Marc. He has asthma. I came to give the children checkups. I have presents for them."

"Presents," the male voice repeated in Spanish. "*Sí.*"

He whistled and the dogs vanished into the trees and an older man stepped out on the porch. His smile was inviting and friendly.

"Eliza told me about you," he said in Spanish. "What did you bring today?"

Shayla pulled out a bag of balloons. Her Spanish was

improving, but was not as good as Jake's, who interpreted for her.

"I'll give the kids balloons after I examine them. Deal?"

"Like for a birthday party?" he asked.

"*Sí.*" She blew up one and twisted it into a dog.

He took it. "This is good. *Gracias.*"

Children with interested eyes looked at her. "Welcome, Doctor Crawford, I am Rico Gonzales. We are glad you are here."

Shayla answered in Spanish. "*Gracias,* Senor Gonzales. May we come in?"

"*Sí.*"

Five eager faces greeted her and Jake. "You have a large family, Senor."

He shook his head. "My grandchildren," he corrected. "My kids are working. Rosalie"—he gestured toward the hallway—"she's not feeling well. I watch them while she is sick."

"Anything serious?" Jake asked.

"My wife says she is blue. Depressed. I don't know."

Shayla hooked on her stethoscope and gave the extra one she carried to the first child who approached. Senor Gonzales called him Tony. Shayla caught his eye and gestured for him to listen to Dr. Jake's heartbeat.

Jake was examining a little girl with the most expressive eyes Shayla had ever seen. She followed Jake's hands with innocent trust that Shayla found absolutely endearing.

Tony tapped her knee. She pointed her thumb down.

He pointed his thumb down.

"Doctor Parker is dead?" she asked.

The boy nodded and everyone laughed.

The men conversed in Spanish and English and

Shayla followed what she could of the two languages. Jake and Mr. Gonzales laughed like old friends.

Shayla lifted a bruiser of a little boy onto her lap and grunted. "You're a big guy."

Senor Gonzales waved his hand and looked as if he'd given up on the kid. "He eats all the children's food. We have to watch that one."

Juan was heavy, but quick. He was also in perfect health. He jumped from her lap and into Senor Gonzales's.

Shayla twisted another balloon dog and gave it to Juan, who promptly bit it.

"You know any more animals?" Senor Gonzales asked.

Her nose wrinkled. "No."

"That is okay. Dogs are good, too."

Jake worked efficiently, recording information on the new sheets that Pearline had given them. The exams took little time, but the questions from the children took more.

Why did Shayla speak Spanglish?

Where were her children? Why did she have on a dress? When would she come see them again? Could they come with her?

Shayla answered them all, laughing and soothing them when she had to administer the shots. She twisted dog balloons until her fingers were pinched and red, but the children were happy. She gave each one a licorice and their very own flash cards that Jessie had packed.

Jake talked as they worked and then asked to see Rosalie.

Shayla followed the men to Rosalie's room.

The woman greeted them with a smile. "Doctor Parker," she said in Spanish, "how are you today?"

"Fine, but it's you I'm worried about."

"I'm sure my father did a terrible job explaining my sickness."

"You will feel better if you get up," Senor Gonzales said. "Maybe you can get her out of bed. Ah." He threw up his hands and left to check on the kids.

Shayla tiptoed closer to the bed. "Hi, I'm Doctor Crawford. What do you hope for, a boy or girl?"

Rosalie smiled. "I want a girl, but my husband wants a boy to rough around with."

Shayla slid onto the bed and gently took her hand. "I have a little brother who's four. He's pretty rough."

"*Sí,* you?"

Shayla had seen the look many times. "My mother and father can't seem to stay away from each other. I didn't punish them enough as a kid."

Rosalie touched her hand. "You look like you were a sweet girl."

Shayla laughed, enjoying Rosalie's easy manner. "I was a terrorist, trust me. My brother is worse, I'm glad to say. So what's really bothering you?"

Rosalie's gaze shifted to Jake, who stood at the foot of the bed. "You want me to leave? We were just getting to the good part."

Both women laughed at Jake's burst of humor. *Who knew?* Shayla thought. She turned back to Rosalie. "He's safe. What's going on?"

Her expression saddened. "My husband was deported last week and I don't know if he'll make it back before the baby is born. This is our first child."

Rosalie's hand closed around a framed photo, and Shayla took it. The smiling man had his hands around Rosalie's expanding waist. They looked like they were very much in love. "Wow, you guys are sure in love."

This brought giggles from Rosalie. "Of course we are. I want him home with me."

"Is there a possibility that he could come back legally?"

"Not unless someone sponsors him. My father was going to, but he lost his job at the hotel when tourism dropped off."

"What does your husband do?"

"He was a tree surgeon in our native Cuba."

"Wow. That's very cool," Shayla said and smiled.

"You never met the wife of a tree surgeon before?"

"No, I never met a tree surgeon before either. I was sheltered," Shayla said, shaking her head pitifully.

Rosalie laughed and playfully pinched Shayla's arm. "You are too much."

"I know a few people who'd agree with you there. Are you going to be a stay-at-home mom, Rosalie?"

"No, I hope to work in a doctor's office as I have before."

Shayla started to smile. "You were a physician, weren't you?"

Rosalie's grin was genuine. "You are the first person to ever ask instead of assume I was there to clean the building. Yes, I was."

"You've got intelligent eyes and an easy disposition. Plus, I knew you were taking my pulse a minute ago."

The two women cracked up, and Jake finally closed his mouth.

"Rosalie," Jake said, "how long have I known you, two years, and you never told me you're a doctor?"

"I don't advertise, Doctor Jake. I can't afford the attention right now."

Shayla clasped Rosalie's hand. "Things will work out."

Shayla repositioned the picture on the stand so Rosalie could see him. "I wonder what your husband would say if he knew you were wallowing in bed."

"He'd want to be here, of course!"

"I'm leaving," Jake said.

Shayla and Rosalie burst out laughing as Jake double-timed it out of the room. "So that's how you get rid of him. Do you mind if I finish the exam?"

"No, go ahead."

They chatted like old friends and Shayla reported a strong heartbeat and a healthy kick from the baby. "You're fine and so is the baby."

Rosalie's face clouded. "We don't have money to pay you."

Shayla folded the stethoscope. "We'll barter."

"I don't have anything."

"I saw jelly and jams stored out on the shelf. I would love to have one."

"Doctor, you're cheating yourself. It is very easy to make yourself. The berries are sweet and ripe now."

"You haven't seen me in the kitchen. Restaurants were created for people like me."

"Come on." Rosalie didn't believe her. "Your mama did not teach you how to cook? I thought all black girls knew how to cook."

Shayla laughed at that. "Well, meet the first sista tossed out of the kitchen for burning up the pots."

A rosy glow surfaced in Rosalie's cheeks. "You are a spoiled girl. How long have you been here?"

"Four months."

"What have you eaten for four months?"

"Ravioli."

Rosalie's mouth hung open. "What does Doctor Parker have to say about that? He watches you so intently, I would swear he knew how many breaths you take in a minute."

"I got a little sick on the way over here."

"You know what I'm talking about. He's got *that* look."

Shayla didn't want to go there. "He thinks I should eat more ravioli and stay out of his way. I'd better get going. Will you come see me at the center? I only take jelly as payment."

Rosalie touched her arm affectionately. "You are good people, Doctor Crawford."

"You too, Doctor Rosalie . . ."

"Menendez. I will come see you in three weeks." Rosalie's eyes twinkled. "Perhaps I will probably need the rest of the day in bed to recuperate, no?"

Shayla winked at her. "You bet."

"Thank you for coming, Doctor Crawford. Will you send my father back in?"

Shayla walked back into the kitchen. Jake had masking tape all over his arms and pant legs from the children making play bandages.

Mr. Gonzalez snoozed in the chair in the living room.

"Kids," Jake said in Spanish, "go tell Grandfather I am leaving."

Mr. Gonzalez awoke and looked grateful. "I get no rest. These kids."

Jake gave him a bag of medication. "Keep this blood pressure medication away from the children. There're enough samples for a month. Come see me when you run out."

"Senor, Rosalie would like to see you."

"*Gracias.* You're too kind. *Uno momento,*" he said and went to see what Rosalie wanted.

He hurried out with two jars of jelly. "Don't forget. Rosalie will bring more in three weeks."

"*Gracias.* It was a pleasure to meet you."

"*De nada*. You have done us a great favor coming here. Rosalie looks much better."

Mr. Gonzales whistled off the dogs and watched in shock as Shayla climbed on and they rode away.

By eight that night, Shayla couldn't feel her butt.

Jake pulled around the back of her cabin and cut off the engine.

Easing her head off his shoulder, she opened her tired eyes. "Shouldn't we stop at the center and drop this stuff off?"

"I'll do it."

She didn't have the strength to argue. Shayla's legs felt unnaturally wide as she struggled to get them both on the same side of the bike. Modesty gone, she threw her right over and braced her knees until she felt them start to burn.

"You made it," he said softly.

Only then did she stagger up the stairs. "Doctor Parker, I think you're admitting that I accomplished the unthinkable." Keys in hand, she turned the lock.

"Which is?" he said easily.

"I impressed you. After that one minor incident, which will never be mentioned again, I was wonderful."

"Please, be more full of yourself," he teased, stepping up behind her.

"A fact is a fact. You're shocked that I made it this far."

Shayla pushed open the door just as a figure emerged from her bedroom.

Shayla screamed and fell backward.

Twelve

Jake caught Shayla in his arms just as Jessie hurried to the front door. "Doctor Crawford, it's just me."

Shayla turned and looked up. "Jessie, you scared me to death! What are you doing here?"

"Do you want to come inside?"

Shayla slid away from Jake. "Sorry."

"Not a problem," he said.

They walked inside and Shayla groped for the light. "Jessie? What's going on?"

The young nurse emerged from the shadows just as the kitchen light flooded the room. The harsh overhead light showed the bruises on her face.

"Good grief, what happened?" Shayla walked gingerly on her sore feet and pulled Jessie into the kitchen. She shoved her into the chair and tilted up her chin. "Who did this?"

"Pierce and I had a fight."

"Your husband?"

"Yes."

"He'd better be in jail," Jake said.

"He is."

Shayla examined Jessie's cheekbones and accepted peroxide and cotton balls from Jake. "I hope he looks worse than you."

"I can't hit an old man."

"Why? Does he have an invisible force field you can't penetrate?"

"No—"

"No nothing, Jessie. You're entitled to respect, and if your husband treats you like this, you have no business being with him."

Jessie's eyes watered, but Shayla had seen too much abuse at every hospital she'd ever worked in. "How old is old?"

"Forty-eight."

"He's older than my father." What would she see in a man of that age?

"Yeah, I know." Jessie winced when Shayla pressed the ice on her face.

"Were you looking for me when you came here?"

"Jake," she said. "I couldn't get in his house, the door was locked. Then I stopped over here to see if you were back but I had to use the bathroom. I was coming out when you were coming in. Sorry I scared you."

"How did you get in?"

"I had a key from when I cleaned the cabin before you came. I forgot to give it back to Jake. I'm sorry. I didn't mean to invade your privacy."

"Hey, hey." Shayla sank into the chair next to Jessie. "I don't care about the key. In fact, keep it. You can come over here anytime. Understand?"

"Thanks."

"I'm sorry too, sweetie," Jake said to Jessie. "I locked the door because I've had intruders lately."

Shayla gave him the evil eye. "Why don't you stay here tonight? We can eat ice cream and watch TV."

Jessie tried to smile, but her fleshy lip dragged over her teeth and ended in a painful grimace. "Thank you, Doctor Crawford, but I don't want to bring my problems into your home."

"I haven't met a problem I couldn't handle."

"If it's all the same, I'll sleep in Jake's spare room tonight." She got up, and Shayla couldn't help but notice how frail she was. Jake handed over the key and grabbed her hands.

"It's a damned good thing Pierce is already in jail." He kissed Jessie's forehead. "Don't worry. We won't let anything happen to you."

"Thank you both." Impulsively, she hugged Jake, then Shayla.

"Wait." Shayla quickly dug under the sink. She pulled out a flashlight and a stun gun.

Jessie took both. "What's this?"

"It's a stun gun." Taking the instrument from Jessie's hand, she demonstrated by pressing the button on one of the sofa cushions.

The crackling sound was convincing. "Press this on man or beast, and it'll stop them cold. Then you can get away."

"Wow." Jessie was clearly awed. "I've never seen anything like this in my whole life."

"You should come to my aunt and uncle's house sometime. They have some very cool stuff."

"Really?"

Shayla walked Jessie to the door. "Really. If you change your mind, come on back."

"Okay. Good night." Shayla and Jake hovered in the

doorway like parents watching their young. When the light popped on at Jake's, they sat down.

"How long has that been going on?"

"About six months. She married him to please her father and now her father's dead. Pierce wanted a maid and he got a woman who won't bend to his will."

"Good for Jessie." Shayla didn't have the stomach for men who abused women or the women who stayed. "Hopefully she won't go back. So, is this good night?"

"I'll stay only a minute."

"Suit yourself. I'm having dinner." Shayla dug out a knife, bread, peanut butter, and the jelly from Rosalie's, and collapsed in a chair. Her feet hurt, her back hurt, and her neck hurt. She would have included her legs and teeth, but she needed both for separate reasons. "Want one?" Shayla pulled two pieces of bread from the bag and bit into her sandwich.

Jake shook his head.

"Suit yourself. This is so good. Ow. Ow. Ow." She dragged her legs forward. "I should be in bed eating so I don't have to go anywhere when I fall asleep."

Jake pulled her legs onto his lap. "You need the right equipment if you're going to survive in the Delta."

"Hey! Just what do you think you're doing?"

He peeled her ruined shoes from her feet. "These are the wrong shoes." He tossed one, then the other into the garbage.

"My feet don't have that fresh-after-the-bath smell, so would you kindly not ruin my dinner and let them go?"

"Your feet don't smell." Jake pressed his fingers into each toe and worked tension and pain out of the swollen limbs.

"You must have powerful allergies not to smell these things."

"Shh. Eat."

Shayla chewed slowly, stripes of relief shooting up her leg. Her head lolled back and she sighed.

"Do you have any sneakers?" he said quietly.

"Hmm? Yes," she moaned, her eyes now closed.

"Wear them tomorrow with pants."

Shayla's eyes fluttered as his fingers touched the inflamed bug bites on her leg. "Put cortisone cream on these. And the medicine I gave you for the poison ivy."

Unwilling to break the silence by reminding him she was a licensed doctor, Shayla let his fingers console her aching muscles.

His hands worked up to her calf and Shayla tensed. So far he hadn't touched her knees, an erogenous zone she'd discovered by accident when her cousin's dog licked her.

But as Jake's hands circled her kneecaps, a resulting shiver curled up her legs, moving toward the center of her body.

Stimulated with no possibility of relief, Shayla tried to retrieve her feet.

"Be still." The command was issued like the military order "atten-tion!" Shayla didn't move a muscle, instead redirecting her brain on the impersonal nature of his touch.

But try as she might, she couldn't make the shift.

Instead, she became more aware of the meeting of his palms against her legs, the cuff of his shirt in the wake of his fingers.

Each sensation produced separate but equal pleasures until she had to move or give herself to him.

Jake's eyes met hers. "What is it, Shayla?"

His fingers slid from her heel to the ball of her foot

and breezed over her toes. Ripples shot up her leg. "If you must know, my toes are highly erogenous."

She tried again to reclaim her foot, but Jake palmed her heel, stroking just her pinky toe. A firecracker would have sent her into orbit, she was that sensitive.

Jake knew exactly where to touch to have her completely at his will. So Shayla forced herself to watch him. Her breath hissed as he moved over each toe.

"This is unfair," she said. Jake raised his eyebrows at the husky statement. "You know something incredibly personal about me," she said, "and I don't know anything about you."

"You're talkative and I'm not." In his strong hand, he grasped her other leg, bringing it to his lap.

"I can't believe I'm letting you touch my feet." She brought her head up and rested her temple on her finger. "You know what I think, Jake?"

He shook his head.

"I think you have a foot fetish." A sexy grin split his mouth. "You love women's feet so much, you only see patients with feet problems."

"Interesting, but wrong." Working each toe, he eased pain away, replaced by a tension that could only be relieved when all her toes were curled together at ecstasy's door.

Slowly his hands moved up her legs. "You wear women's shoes when nobody's around."

He'd flattened her foot against his chest, and his chuckle vibrated through her body. Teasing fingers made her knees quiver.

"Gay," he said, "and wrong." Once again his hands slowed at her knees.

When she looked into his eyes, his intent was unmistakable and the light clicked on. "You're trying to seduce me."

"Bingo."

Jake clasped the hand she'd been leaning on, and pulled her forward. Just as he'd deliberately soothed every inch of her foot, he did with her mouth also.

Shayla couldn't remember ever having been kissed so thoroughly.

Jake seduced her with his tongue, like a *sensei* used weapons for defense.

It had been so long since she'd been held or kissed, Shayla returned the ardor with passion of her own. Jake wanted her. *Wanted her.* And she wanted him.

Their mutual desire tripped a caution switch in her brain. This was Jake. *Jake.*

Shayla broke the kiss and struggled to find her equilibrium.

"What are you doing?" she asked point-blank.

His eyes slid open and she looked at his moist mouth. "I thought you knew."

"I don't, Jake. Are you planning to make love to me and then turn against me tomorrow?"

His eyes moved to hers, and cleared. "Nothing at work has anything to do with me finding you attractive."

A cool breeze whistled under the door. "It has everything to do with it for me."

"There are Epsom salts under your bathroom sink. Take a long soak. Good night."

Shayla walked on the sides of her aching feet. "Why are you running?" she demanded. "A minute ago you had your tongue down my throat and now you're ready to go?"

Jake's eyebrows twitched. "If this were just about sleeping with you, Shayla, I would have tried to seduce you the week you got here."

This surprised her. "Really?"

"Don't act like you don't know the effect you have

on men. All day long, men were running after you like
you had a steak taped to your butt. No stockings and
long, very pretty legs? You knew."

She chuckled at that.

"But it's not about that, but where we come from.
You graduated from Emory. You wear clothes nobody
here can afford and you look at life through rose-
colored glasses."

She couldn't refute him. "Even if you knew my story,
I'd still offer the same advice. This isn't about me or
you."

"It is. I don't come from a society that takes and
gives money easily. Frankly, rich people are too much
trouble."

"Jake, I wondered why you were pushing every idea
away, and I just realized why. You don't want to be
rejected."

"Who does?"

She moved away from the door and walked into her
bedroom.

Jake was watching. As he said, he'd been watching
men watch her all day. "You remind me of a child who
no longer believes in Santa Claus. I'm going to show
you there's goodness in those that give to others. Good
night, Jake."

Shayla closed the bathroom door and started the
water in the tub.

The outside door clicked behind him as he went
home.

Thirteen

Jake Parker had the resolve of a pit bull. No matter what Shayla tried, he remained as elusive and distant as a human to a skunk.

Shayla enlisted the help of Major Spears, and men like Mr. Gonzalez and his sons, who volunteered to paint the center's exterior in thanks for taking such good care of Eliza and Rosalie.

Shayla had thought her actions would rile Jake, but he'd greeted the men with warm handshakes and even took his lunch break with them, but gave Shayla no more than a distant acknowledgment.

By the end of the hot summer months, Shayla felt her mood shift like the once vibrant leaves. Her pattern of rising early, working until she staggered back to her cabin, and filling up on canned ravioli had gotten old.

And Jake's nonresponsiveness was enough to depress even the most optimistic person.

She cracked her neck and swung her arms across her chest. "Ow."

Her joints ached from lack of exercise. This rare Saturday off was a blessing. Shayla had no intention of sitting around just because she had nothing better to do.

She looked out the kitchen window and noticed how many leaves had shed during the night.

Gusty winds increased, preparing the land for winter.

Squirrels busied themselves on the naked branches, and as Shayla watched a pair her gaze drifted over to Jake's cabin.

The lights were off. She couldn't tell if he was there or not. To her dismay, he remained a mystery.

The night of their kiss flitted through her mind, and that "something good has happened to me" feeling engulfed her, followed closely by emptiness and disappointment. Jake had kissed her so long ago she couldn't help but wonder if he'd forgotten that he'd wanted to take her to bed.

Am I that forgettable?

She wrapped her arms around her waist and squeezed. Her mouth dropped open.

Were those love handles?

When was the last time she'd bounced a basketball or chased a tennis ball?

Shayla stripped and stared at her naked body in the bathroom mirror. When had she gained weight?

For the past three months she'd subsisted mostly on ravioli.

And cereal her patients brought as a treat.

And candy she used to bribe kids into letting her examine them.

And the delicious snack plates the Gonzalez family prepared for her each time she visited Rosalie.

And no exercise.

The full curve of her breasts filled her palms.

Was that a dip?

If she kept this up, they'd be on the floor by spring!

Yanking on her workout clothes, Shayla rummaged through the closet.

When she'd come into the Crawford family, she'd integrated the male-only basketball games and brought the women from the sidelines to the court. Now two of her uncles refereed, the hustle too intense for them. Shayla grabbed her basketball, liking the feel of the hard rubber against her hand.

She wasn't Sheryl Swoops, but she had a little game.

Jessie had pointed out a court near Natchez, and had mentioned in passing that Jake used to play on Saturdays.

Shayla was on the road in no time flat. If Jake wouldn't come to her, she'd go to him.

The court was full of early morning risers. Older men played on one end, while the younger guys played on the other.

There was only one female on the court and Shayla hoped to even out the odds. Jake wasn't there, but who knew if he'd show at all? Even if he didn't, she'd still get in some exercise. She walked down and waited.

"You lost, lady?"

The guy with the least amount of game swaggered up to her and checked out her matching Nike shoes, shorts, and T-shirt. He pointed to her socks with the signature check mark and dropped back, snickering. "You're definitely lost. The aerobics gym is in Jackson."

She bounced her regulation-size ball. "I came to play."

He doubled over laughing. Shayla hated guys like him. "Baby, you too pretty to be out here."

"You're going to mess up your makeup," another guy added.

So what that she'd put on a little lipstick while in the car? It had sunscreen in it! Anyway, bigmouth number two's outside shot was weak. "That's my problem, isn't it?"

"The only girl that's got any game is Kris, so she's the only one we let play."

"Is that Kris?" The young woman Shayla pointed to wore dreads, her stance all boy. The ball she tossed was all net. Kris was a ballplayer.

"Yep."

"Well, we'll see what Kris has to say about a game against you two."

Shayla headed over to the woman, who gave her a curious look.

"Hey, sista," Kris greeted her and slapped Shayla's palm. "These boys trying to run you down?"

"They won't let me play, but I thought you and I could teach them a few things."

Kris's eyebrows shot up. "Can you play?"

Shayla sized up her potential partner. Up close, Kris was about five-eight and had good definition in her arms and legs. She looked like a real athlete, not just a girl hanging out tryin' to be cute. "I got a little game," Shayla answered her.

The men oohed and laughed.

Kris sat on her ball, perspiration soaking her headband. "I don't know. I usually play with the doc over there, and take on a couple of these fools, just for fun."

Shayla saw Jake before he saw her. Her heart began to race.

"I wondered if he'd show."

"What was that?"

Shayla hurried on. "How about us three against"—she pointed to the two men who'd said she couldn't play—"these three?"

Kris rose and bounced her ball. "You got guts. Okay, let's do it. Hey, Doc?" Kris yelled. "You're with us."

Jake jogged over and did a double take when he saw Shayla. "What are you doing here?"

"Same as you, apparently."

"Hey, Doc," Kris said. "Meet—what's your name?"

"Shayla."

"I know her," Jake muttered. "She's the new doctor at the center."

"You said you were getting somebody, but I thought you said it was a man."

"That's what I thought."

"Please." Shayla didn't hide her distaste. "Talk about me like I'm not here." She stared Jake in the eye. "You here to play ball or what?"

"It's your neck."

"Let's get this party started," Kris said, and the court cleared.

"Who chose them?" Jake asked, giving the other team a concerned look.

"I did. Why?" Shayla asked.

"Nothing. We don't play a second game, no matter what."

An uneasy feeling knotted Shayla's stomach, but Kris left the circle swinging her arms across her stomach and cracking her neck.

"I got Shorty. Shay, you got Mixer."

"Who's that?"

Even to her own ears Shayla sounded too proper. The guys on the sidelines mimicked her and laughed.

She'd just play the game and hope for the best. "The dark one with the braids and the white sweat band," Kris said. "Doc, you got Big Boy. We taking the ball out?" she asked the other team.

"Yeah, and that's the last nice thing we gon' do for you," Big Boy said back.

Shayla bounced the ball and went out of bounds. She slapped the ball to signal her team to break and threw it in. Big Boy wasn't slow because of his size. He intercepted and made an easy layup.

The courtside spectators howled with laughter.

Shayla got the ball back, bounced it hard, and tossed. It hit Jake's chest, fell, and Mixer slammed it in.

Kris rolled her eyes and slapped the ball from Mixer's hand as he fell to his knees, laughing.

"Get in the game," she hollered at Shayla.

"Damnit!" Shayla dried her hands on her shorts and listened to her unsteady heartbeat. She licked her lips, unable to catch a rhythm.

Jake nudged her arm. "Don't try so hard."

She fell in step, ignoring the guys that mocked the swing of her hips. She was a better player than this.

Mixer stood in front of her, tall and lanky, but she felt a certain comfort steal over her. Her uncles Edwin and Justin were big men, but one thing she knew was that big men always had a weak side. Mixer tried to inbound the ball, but Shayla used quick hands and slapped it back.

The crowd reacted with surprised yells.

Mixer was still laughing as he retrieved the ball and tried to throw it over her head. Shayla jumped, tapped it back, sending the ball one bounce outside the line.

The smile left Mixer's face as the crowd cheered for her.

Shayla knew he would try something, and when he

aimed the ball at her leg and tried to hit her, she scooped it up easily and tossed it to Jake, who laid it in.

They had finally scored two points.

Kris threw the ball and Shayla caught the sharp pass. "Get it into play this time."

Shayla nodded and kept her eye on Jake. The guys didn't anticipate her pass to Kris until it was in her hands. Kris laid it up for two. The crowd erupted.

They had a ball game.

Shayla hustled hard for her team, scoring eight of their eighteen points.

She scrapped, skinned her knees, and argued when she thought she'd been fouled. A couple of times Jake had to push guys out of her face, she was talking so much trash.

They'd started calling her Gray for her eyes, and now that the game was close the guys from the sidelines were shouting loudly for and against her.

Her team huddled, plotting their defense, while the guys from the other team searched for Shorty's missing contact lens.

Kris barked quiet orders. "Gray, foul Shorty as soon as he gets the ball."

"I'm not fouling him." These guys would think she was a punk who couldn't stand a close game.

"Listen, he can't see without his contact."

"So he'll miss the shot and we'll get the ball." Shayla wasn't going down like that.

"But what if he doesn't miss?"

"Then we lose, but not because I hacked him."

"That's good, Shayla, always the team player," Jake said sarcastically.

"I'm not fouling him," she said louder. She moved center court and waited for the other team.

Jake nudged her as he passed. "Fouling is part of the game."

Shayla didn't even look at him. "Just make sure you keep your eye on Big Boy. You've been a little slow on the post."

"Hello," Kris cooed. "Excuse me, lovebirds, but the game is still going on."

"We are not lovebirds," Shayla said.

"It's not from lack of trying." Jake pushed a stunned Shayla to the guard position.

Shayla was so shocked she almost missed fouling Shorty. He cried out, as if she'd broken his arm. "I should sue. You almost broke my d—"

"Hey," Kris yelled. "No cussing."

"She almost broke my *danged* arm. Now I'm gon' score all in her face," he said with one eye closed.

Everybody lined up.

"Is that your good eye or your bad one?" Shayla asked, right before Shorty shot the ball.

He missed, she rebounded, and shot a jumper for the winning goal.

"She cheated!" Shorty jumped up and down, but the sidelines had cleared and Shayla celebrated with Kris and Jake.

"You're all right," Kris complimented Shayla as the swarm of spectators flowed around them. "You play in college?"

"Nope. Just around the way."

Kris laughed. "You ain't no kind of 'round the way girl I've ever seen. Where did you ball?"

"On the driveway. Really," Shayla assured her.

"Okay." Kris dried off and pulled a band from her hair, releasing a torrent of black locks. Kris was a stunning woman. Shayla wondered if a romance had ever developed between Jake and Kris.

"How long you been here, Gray?"

"Almost seven months."

Kris gave Jake a playful punch in the arm. "Doc, you've been holding out."

Jake's admiring look registered, and goose bumps slid all over Shayla's arms. She gathered her ball and headed up the grassy slope to her car.

The three guys they'd played surrounded her. "Where you going? We want a rematch."

"No."

"She cheated," Shorty argued. "I want a rematch."

"You're such a pro basketball player, I guess people should shut up for you like they do for Shaquille O'Neal. Right?" Shayla walked around Shorty and hit the automatic release button on her trunk.

"Bitch!" he yelled.

Shayla turned, to find Jake chest to chest with the man. "Go home," he said.

Shorty shoved off Jake and started back to the court.

Kris seemed very happy. "You sure know how to make friends."

"It's my all-time talent. I'm a doctor just for kicks."

The two women laughed. "I like you, Shay. Jake, are you coming to the mayor's reception?"

"You work for the mayor?" Shayla asked.

"As his personal executive assistant." Kris stretched her triceps muscles. "Great time to network and schmooze. Who knows, you might get a benefactor to paint that dilapidated building you call a medical center," she joked.

"Had it done a while ago," Shayla said to fill in the stony silence.

"Who? You?" Kris stared between them.

"I bartered with some friends. It's not dingy gray, but

brand-new dingy gray. Was the invitation only for Doctor Parker?''

"No. Two."

"I decline." Jake's expression invited no discussion.

"How about you, Gray?" Kris looked between them until understanding lightened her face. "Ah, I see. I'll go ahead and decline for you both."

Shayla showed Jake her back. "Kris, I'm coming. Do you go to Shiloh?"

"Yep."

"Good. I'll be in church tomorrow. Can you bring it then?"

Kris's eyes twinkled. "Sure. You made the game interesting today. Come back anytime." Kris jogged to her car and took off.

Shayla climbed into the BMW and stabbed the ignition just as Jake opened the passenger door and slid in.

"What do you want?" Jake hadn't said two kind words to her in months. And right now, she was too mad for casual chitchat.

"Drive," he said. "Before your friends come back."

"I can take care of myself, thank you very much. Now get the hell out of my car!"

"Those guys are in the most violent gang in Alberta, and they're pissed off at you."

She was mad, not stupid. "What about your truck?"

"They won't bother it. I'll come back later."

Shayla gunned the engine and drove ten miles before pulling over.

"I'm going to the reception, so you might as well get out now."

"You're not going anywhere near those people," he said.

"Those people? You're so—prejudiced! I'd rather be

around *them*. At least with *them* their prejudice wouldn't surprise me."

"I don't care. You're not going representing the center."

"I'm not only going to represent the center, but you, too. And there's nothing you can do to stop me."

Fourteen

Jake gripped the door as Shayla careened onto the highway, the gauge hitting sixty miles per hour in five seconds flat. She handled the car with the same tenacious spirit that she used to gain her patients' trust, and today on the male-dominated court.

How could he tell her he'd taken her advice and asked for financial support, but had been summarily turned down?

Maybe Shayla's confidence had nothing to do with money. She said she'd been poor. But she'd been young, and children didn't know things until somebody told them differently.

For a week, Jake had been walking around in a fog. The funding earmarked for the center had been diverted into the new hospital.

The poor and low-income people were being punished for not doing better in life. The new facility had broken ground five months ago, but no one had been brave enough to tell him they were being shut down. They'd just taken the money.

"Why is it so hard for you to let somebody else have an idea and help?" Shayla asked him.

"That's not it."

"You act like you're the last known hero."

"You're not from these parts."

Shayla eased off the accelerator and turned onto the interstate. "Do you want me to leave this donor idea alone?"

"Yes."

"Then give me a reason to. Tell me your story, Jake."

Jake didn't know why he was letting himself be dragged into this discussion, but he wanted her to understand. "My grandfather grew up here and served in World War II. He lost a leg for his country and got nothing in return. It wasn't until President Clinton was in office that my grandfather was posthumously awarded a Purple Heart."

"You must have been very proud."

He looked at her with a quick jerk of his eyes. Bittersweet pain filled him. "That was a great day." He cleared his throat.

"My grandfather married, and my mother was born. Shortly after, my grandmother died. Granddad worked with veterans, white and black, helping men deal with the pain of the war. Men didn't talk openly about their feelings back then, but they could hardly turn down a talk from a man with one leg."

"I see."

"Grandfather could find hope in the smallest thing. He told them if he could make it with one leg, they could do anything. Pearline and I followed in our mother's and grandparents' footsteps. My mother became a midwife, and Pearline an LPN, and me a doctor."

"That's pretty amazing."

"Yeah. I don't care about color, money, or status, but I'm not begging for help."

"Jake, don't you ever get tired of the burden?"

He wanted to admit to being weary, but his grandfather had never complained. "Surrendering isn't going to save a single life."

"You aren't the last angel, Jake. People want to help."

"I'm not like you, Shayla. I've stopped looking for needles in haystacks. I'm here, and for now you're here."

"Yes, I am."

Jake submitted to her intense scrutiny. When her gray gaze returned to the road, he realized she'd filled him ocean-deep with compassion.

She'd used the only decoder to what was locked inside him.

A mountain of burden shifted on his shoulders, and Jake's mind cleared until only one thought occupied the space.

He'd denied himself this pleasure for so long. He wanted to touch her. Some sixty or so doctors had come through the Alberta center and none had reached beyond themselves to touch the patients, let alone him. Shayla had her hands firmly gripped around him, but Jake wasn't sure if he could ever follow her lead.

Gold earrings clung to her ears like a lover's lip. They whispered *expensive*.

Her brand-name shirt, expensive.

The little vehicle they sat in, expensive.

Even her regulation basketball, expensive.

Shayla was the diamond to his rough.

Although he told himself not to want her, his mind and body begged for her. Would there ever be a time when he didn't feel inferior to her?

Shayla parked and looked at him. "What are you thinking right now? And don't lie to me."

Longing shook his empty soul. "I was thinking if we were in a different time, we'd be good together."

"You've avoided me since our kiss. What changed today?"

"You, on the court. I saw a part of you I'd never seen before. I've misjudged you." He chuckled softly. "You surprised me, again."

"Excited you," she filled in the unspoken words.

"Yes."

"Then what makes you think I'm so unobtainable?"

He took her hand and touched the dainty gold and diamond-encrusted bracelet. "I couldn't give you the things you deserve."

"Is that it? You're worried about *things?* That's superficial and sad."

Her words pounded at him. Especially since patients often put doctors on pedestals and when they couldn't afford care, they'd go sick rather than admit they couldn't pay.

But he understood them better than he did her. "Shayla, I'm sitting in a forty-thousand-dollar car, one I couldn't afford on what I make in three years. It's lifestyle," he told her. "You're counting the days until you can leave. Aren't you?"

"Is that why you won't touch me? Why sometimes you won't even speak to me?"

"I didn't realize—" he said, but couldn't finish. What she'd said was true.

"You're hurting every patient I can't get a consultation on because you shut me out. I'm a smart doctor, a good doctor. But I don't know everything. You're proving two adults can't be attracted to each other and work together."

3 QUICK STEPS
TO RECEIVE YOUR "THANK YOU" GIFT
FROM THE EDITOR

Send this card back and you'll receive 4 FREE Arabesque novels! The introductory shipment of 4 Arabesque novels – a $23.96 value – is yours absolutely FREE!

There's no catch. You're under no obligation to buy anything. You'll receive your introductory shipment of 4 Arabesque novels absolutely FREE (plus $1.50 to offset the costs of shipping & handling). And you don't have to make any minimum number of purchases—not even one!

We hope that after receiving your books you'll want to remain an Arabesque subscriber. But the choice is yours to continue or cancel, anytime at all! So why not take us up on our invitation to receive 4 Arabesque Romance Novels, with no risk of any kind. You'll be glad you did!

Call us
TOLL-FREE
at 1-800-770-1963

THE EDITOR'S "THANK YOU" GIFT INCLUDES:

- 4 books absolutely FREE (plus $1.50 for shipping and handling)
- A FREE newsletter, *Arabesque Romance News*, filled with author interviews, book previews, special offers, and more!
- No risks or obligations. You're free to cancel whenever you wish... with no questions asked.

BOOK CERTIFICATE

Yes! Please send me 4 FREE Arabesque novels (plus $1.50 for shipping & handling). I understand I am under no obligation to purchase any books, as explained on the back of this card.

Name _____

Address _____ Apt. _____

City _____ State _____ Zip _____

Telephone ( ) _____

Signature _____

Offer limited to one per household and not valid to current subscribers. All orders subject to approval. Terms, offer, & price subject to change. Offer valid only in the U.S.

Thank you!

AN052A

Accepting the four introductory books for FREE (plus $1.50 to offset the cost of shipping & handling) places you under no obligation to buy anything. You may keep the books and return the shipping statement marked "cancelled". If you do not cancel, about a month later we will send 4 additional Arabesque novels, and you will be billed the preferred subscriber's price of just $4.00 per title. That's $16.00 for all 4 books for a savings of 33% off the cover price (Plus $1.50 for shipping and handling). You may cancel at any time, but if you choose to continue, every month we'll send you 4 more books, which you may either purchase at the preferred discount price. . . or return to us and cancel your subscription.

THE ARABESQUE ROMANCE CLUB: HERE'S HOW IT WORKS

ARABESQUE ROMANCE BOOK CLUB
P.O. Box 5214
Clifton NJ 07015-5214

PLACE
STAMP
HERE

His belly flopped. "Why didn't you say something?"

"I thought you'd realize it on your own."

"I didn't think it was that obvious."

His gaze absorbed the downward turn of her shoulders. He had made her time in Alberta unbelievably hard. Was it really fear or something worse? Was he a snob? Jake didn't want to think that of himself. That'd mean he'd become what he detested.

He looked around. "Why are we at Wal-Mart?"

"I need a few things." She reached into the backseat and pulled out a Gucci purse.

"From here?" Jake prepared for a tirade. Instead, Shayla closed her lips over his in a sensual kiss that sparked his passion.

Her mouth felt so good. Like a delicacy he hadn't savored.

Jake reached for her, but she'd already pushed her door open and was halfway out.

"You're lucky I'm not like you," she said.

"Say again?" Jake tried to clear his fuzzy mind.

"I don't judge a book by its cover. I know the real treat is inside." She got out of the car and walked into the store.

Shayla talked herself out of going to the reception. Her mother had FedEx'd her dress and accessories, but the delivery had sent the center into a tailspin.

Shayla had been examining twin boys who'd gotten a rash, when she heard the excitement in the waiting room.

She'd ignored it until Dee had knocked on the door and told her a special package had arrived that required her signature.

Every eye was on Shayla as she signed and thanked the driver.

Jake had come out too, but Shayla ignored his questioning gaze, and went back to work.

Ever since she'd kissed him, she'd caught him looking at her at the oddest moments. So she gave him a taste of his own medicine and ignored him.

Hours later, Shayla exited her clean exam room and cut off the lights in the center.

Tonight, she just wanted to rest. Maybe the wind would blow in the right direction and she'd watch a little TV. She could give herself a perm and fix a Long Island iced tea.

Shayla indulged in a bout of homesickness and wished Damon were underfoot and her mother and father off somewhere. But instead she headed to her cabin.

What was the use of going to the reception if nobody cared? She'd heard talk about the new hospital and what it would mean to Alberta, but nobody at the center had said a word. Not even Jake.

He'd taken off before noon, and she hadn't seen him since.

Shayla grew more sullen as she climbed the stairs to her cabin. Rural life was lonely. She missed her friends and wondered how everyone was doing.

Feet pounded behind her, and Shayla turned. "Doctor Crawford, there you are." Jessie ran up to her. "Don't tell me you opened it. Have you?" she asked, excited.

"No, and it's Shayla. I'd love to hear my name once in a while."

"Shayla," Jessie said, "I'll hold the box for you."

"You can have it. I'm not going."

Jessie stopped in her tracks. "How come?"

Shayla opened the door and kicked off her shoes. "I

just want to relax. I thought I'd perm my hair and get mildly drunk."

Jessie looked at her as if she'd descended from Mars. "You've let Jake depress you."

"No, I haven't." Had she?

Jessie followed her inside. "Then how can you think of such a thing? The mayor invited you to his house! My goodness, that's right next to going to the White House."

Shayla tossed the box on the sofa and flopped down beside it.

"It's only a reception. There'll be others. You staying?"

Jessie looked sad. "No, because you're going. Your mom took time to send you this dress and you're being selfish."

"How did you know that?" Shayla hadn't told anyone about her mother.

Jessie looked at her funny. "You said your mother was sending you a box and this is it."

Shayla exhaled and clamped her paranoia. All she needed was for Jake to find out her mother was Lauren Michaels.

"I don't think I'd be very good company for the mayor. Come on, let's play Scrabble."

Jessie pointed her small chin out. "We can play Scrabble any time. You have an appointment at the mayor's house. Please, Shayla?"

How could she deny Jessie's earnest face? "On one condition."

Jessie wrapped Shayla in a big hug and pushed her off the couch.

"Wait. You don't know the terms."

"Okay, what are they?"

"You come with me."

Jessie took a step back. "I—I wasn't invited."

Shayla unbuttoned her shirt and threw it on her bed. She came out of her room fastening her dad's raggedy robe. "I just invited you."

"You can't do that."

"Yes, I certainly can," she lied. "It's done all the time. You'll be my guest."

Jessie laughed as if the possibility was too crazy to consider. "No."

Shayla popped the top on a can of soda and drank. "Then I'm not going. Ooh, we can make daiquiris."

"You have to go!"

"Peach or strawberry? We can pop popcorn the old-fashioned way and order—uh—"

Jessie looked at her strangely.

"Pickup," Shayla said. There was no such thing as pizza delivery in this part of Mississippi. "Right, we can make tuna sandwiches and have chips."

"Shay-laa," Jessie whined.

She increased Jessie's anxiety when she picked up the remote and flipped the fuzzy channels. "Would you like to open the box?"

Jessie giggled. "Can I?"

"Only if you say you'll go."

"Doctor Crawford, you're mean and very sneaky."

"I know, my dear." She added fuel to the fire. "I told my mother to send two dresses so I'd have a choice. I can send this home unopened. I wonder if they gave me a return label. No matter," she said and caught the faint view of Vanna White turning letters on the TV screen.

"I want to open it," Jessie whispered desperately.

"Say you'll go." Shayla gave her the box.

"I'll go!"

Jessie ripped into the box and gasped as a black

spaghetti-strap dress fell into her hands. A moan slipped past her lips as she ran her fingers over the soft material.

She glanced at Shayla, her eyes wide. "This is so beautiful. Oh!" She suddenly searched her lap and the couch. Her eyes drooped and she gave the dress to Shayla. "She only sent one. You go, Doctor Crawford."

Now, more than ever, Shayla wanted Jessie to go. For a brief second, all Jessie's troubles had vanished and her face was free of worry and stress. Shayla wanted her to have that moment again.

"I could have sworn I asked her to send my lavender dress."

Shayla upended the box, and a lump of white tissue paper fell out. A Tiffany's box toppled out after it.

Shayla stuck her fingers into the thin paper and withdrew her favorite Vera Wang dress.

Jessie hopped up. "Oh my. My, my, mymymy. I'm going!" She jumped up and down as if she'd won a million dollars.

"Then we'd better get ready." Shayla giggled at Jessie. "You shower first, and I'll hang these to steam. Then we do makeup, hair, and our Cinderella behinds are going to the ball!"

"Thank you." Jessie dashed into the bathroom.

Shayla's foolish smile faded as soon as the door closed. Jake wouldn't be there.

Fifteen

Jake walked into the home of Mayor Dobbs King and forced himself to nod a polite hello to the cheerful attendant. If Shayla wasn't so damned stubborn, he could be at home watching football. But no, he was at the mayor's house, in a new suit and too-tight new shoes.

He needed a moment to get his attitude together.

He strolled through the halls of the mansion, the austere beauty leaving him cold. There had to be something wrong when a public servant lived a hundred times better than the community he served.

"Well, look what the cat dragged in." Kris kissed Jake's cheek.

"You invited me."

"You said you weren't coming."

"Changed my mind. You look nice."

Kris laughed. "I look like a girl, is that it?"

"Will I be in trouble if I say yes?"

"Have you been in trouble for saying the wrong thing lately?"

He snagged a glass from a passing waiter. "Women are exceptional mind readers."

"That we are."

"So, where's your deadbeat boss?"

Kris didn't take offense. "Taking care of last-minute business, so I can hang around for a minute. Want me to introduce you?"

Pearls, diamonds, gold, and platinum floated by him on the richest people of the state. Not one looked his way and he'd met most of them before. "Don't bother."

Anger dimmed the sparkle in Kris's eyes. "Things work out if you know your rights."

"What are you talking about?"

Kris looked away. "I'm restricted by a privacy agreement to keep confidential all matters concerning the office of the mayor."

The assistant district attorney and his wife greeted Kris and she performed introductions. "Pleasure," Jake mumbled, but couldn't wait to get Kris alone. The couple walked off and he guided Kris to the buffet table. "Give me a hint what you're talking about." He selected jumbo shrimp, a plate and napkin.

Kris snagged an olive and chewed as if she just tasted heaven.

"I've said enough. By the way, my feelings aren't hurt that you never fought over me."

He knew this would come up sooner or later. He and Kris had never been romantically linked, but he could see how his behavior with Shayla had raised a red flag. "I'd fight for you. You know that."

The room quieted as the mayor entered. Two beautiful women walked with Mayor King and his wife.

"Well, looky here," Kris murmured. "The doctor cleans up nicely."

Jake watched in stunned silence as Mayor Dobbs King kept quiet council with Shayla. They looked intense, until she laughed, delight brightening her face. The mayor laughed too and shook her hand.

"At least somebody from your neck of the woods has manners," Kris said and joined her boss.

Once again, Shayla wreaked havoc on his mind. She looked like a fairy princess, adorned in fine fabric and jewels.

Her smile attracted men and women and her demeanor exuded class.

The deputy mayor approached Shayla, a man known for his stony manner. He suddenly beamed. Jake took it like a punch to the chest.

Shayla was comfortable with these people. Jake wasn't.

While Jessie fidgeted with her earrings, Shayla never once touched the silver and diamond choker that encircled her neck, but she was aware of her friend and never let Jessie fall into her shadow.

Jake thought about approaching them, but he'd only drag them into his funk. He turned to leave when Shayla fixed her gaze on him.

The sexual tension he'd ignored for months drew them close. Pride shimmered in her eyes and touched him from a distance.

Jake had tuned out the mayor until he said, "Will Doctor Shayla Crawford and Jessie Hathaway please step forward?"

Jake watched the procession with guarded interest.

"Just as we're celebrating the success of new businesses joining our family of flourishing enterprises in Mississippi, I would be remiss if I didn't admit we could improve the work we do in our own backyard. These two ladies work at the Alberta Medical Center. They are angels of mercy."

Applause sprinkled throughout the crowd. "They need more than our sympathy or kind words, they need our financial help."

Hot seething anger rippled through Jake. King had stolen their funding and now was making a public appeal to ingratiate himself to the donors?

"We're so grateful for your support, Mayor King," Shayla said, smoothly stepping into his light. "Under the leadership of Doctor Jake Parker we serve many of the poor or lower-income residents of this fine state. It's our duty to help everyone, but we need your help. The staff at Alberta Medical Center thanks you for this opportunity, and asks that you give generously. Good evening."

The crowd applauded and checks were suddenly being thrust into Shayla's and Jessie's hands.

Jake was dumbfounded. How often had he asked these very same people for support? One hundred times? Two hundred?

This night was a slap in the face. Jake had reached the door just as Shayla touched him. "Mayor King." Her voice rang out loud and strong. "I'd like to introduce you to the doctor that runs the Alberta Medical Center. Doctor Jake Parker."

"Jake, good to see you again."

Not Dr. Parker or even Doctor. Just Jake. *No respect.* "Dobbs, good to see you, too."

The pompous man's eyes widened. "Having a good time this evening?"

Jake smirked. "Duty calls. I've got to make it an early night."

TV cameras swarmed them. "Doctor Parker." Shayla steered them into the bright light. "I've taken the liberty of inviting the mayor and the TV stations for a tour of our facility next Thursday. He's agreed, haven't you, sir?''

The man blushed, practically eating out of Shayla's hands.

"I'd be honored, Doctor Crawford." King laughed jovially and squeezed Jake's hand.

"It would really help the constituents if you released the funding for the center so we can keep our doors open another year."

King's handshake intensified. "I'm working on initiatives that affect all of our citizens. This time next year, we'll have a brand-new facility that will serve everyone."

Jake increased the pressure of their handshake in degrees, until King's eyes nearly popped. "Yes, but forty to sixty miles is too far to travel for some of the patients we see. Especially the young or elderly or handicapped. Would you mind, Mr. Mayor, making a good-faith donation that will show our citizens that you're taking our proposal under advisement, and help those less fortunate than you?''

Jake maneuvered the mayor so the buffet table bursting with food was clearly shown.

There was no clear winner of this showdown of good versus evil.

Jake knew he'd made a powerful enemy, but King had toyed with him for the last time. The mayor leaned toward his wife, who'd remained remarkably calm throughout the entire exchange. The mayor laughed to cover a wince and faced the camera.

"My wife handles the household account and the most she lets me do is shop from a list!" This caused several of the guests to laugh heartily. Jake gave a little tighter squeeze and King assented.

Mrs. King accepted her checkbook from Kris and gave

it to her husband. "Doctor Parker, Alice and I would be honored to present this one-thousand-dollar check to the Alberta Medical Center. Go ahead and take it, young man. This is good money."

Jake didn't reach for the thousand-dollar check. The mayor had made at least half a million dollars tonight. Who was he kidding?

Mrs. King stepped into the camera's lights. "We're giving one thousand dollars and challenge that every interest group represented tonight will match my husband's donation. Starting with me. I will personally give one thousand dollars for myself and each of our four children."

Jake kissed Mrs. King's cheek and she giggled.

King looked furious, but covered well. "It looks as if our campaign fund-raiser has been a blessing to many. If you'd like to donate to either campaign, please send your checks to my office. We'll make sure everything is forwarded to the center."

Jake held up his hands. "Thank you, Mayor, but we don't want your office to allot precious manpower to such a humble project. All donations for the Alberta Medical Center can go to P.O. Box 292 in the Alberta Plaza. Thank you, Mayor King, and your lovely wife. We sincerely appreciate your generosity."

The camera lights slid away and King pulled Jake aside. "What do you think you're doing?" he demanded, furious.

"Seeing how it felt to be mayor?"

"The hospital is going to shut your rinky-dink operation down. Whatever money you raise tonight isn't going to matter. The state owns the land that dilapidated building sits on, thanks to your grandfather."

"I own that land," Jake snapped back.

King took pleasure in stumping Jake. "You might

have a medical degree, but you're not too bright. Go ahead, take the money you get tonight. That'll be the last you see.''

King merged into a sea of his friends, who congratulated him and offered their support. Mrs. King walked over to Jake and extended both hands.

''Ma'am, you've been a generous hostess. Thank you,'' he said.

''Doctor Parker, you're most welcome.'' She guided Jake toward Shayla and Jessie, who were being bombarded with donations. ''I'd like to visit the center on Tuesday. I don't want to get caught in the media crush. Is that all right with you?''

Jake was humbled. ''It would be our pleasure. Have a good evening.''

''Thank you for coming, Doctor Parker.''

Shayla and Jessie appeared at his side, beautiful evening wraps around their shoulders. ''That was a good night's work, wouldn't you say, Doctor Parker?'' Jake touched Shayla for the first time that evening.

Chemistry had been his specialty. What transpired between him and Shayla was a combination of desire, unrequited passion, and curiosity. ''Yes, I would.''

He grabbed Jessie, who had never looked more elegant. ''You're a heart-stopper.''

She blushed. ''Oh, Jake. Thank you.''

He ushered the women to the door.

''You've made a powerful enemy,'' Shayla said, observing King's scowling face as they left the reception.

''I'm not worried about him,'' he said, yet King's words haunted him. Trouble loomed. Jake felt it all the way to his bones.

Sixteen

Shayla sat in Jake's kitchen, the wee morning hours closer to midnight than dawn. The inky darkness created a cove of intimacy where secrets could be shared, then safely tucked behind beating hearts.

Jake had been remarkable tonight.

Intense, and masculine, and damned sexy as he faced his archenemy. His eyes had been feral, his smile beguiling, but beneath the controlled muscles and flesh, a man ready to fight for what he believed in.

Women might be made of sugar and spice, but passion was what real men were made of. Now, Jake moved around his kitchen with ease, making hot chocolate and serving ginger snap cookies.

This was almost Shayla's fantasy come true. Except she'd always imagined champagne, and nothing between her and her partner but air.

Reality departed from fantasy as she sat at Jake's

butcher-block table, her feet propped on the opposite cushioned chair.

Lavender silk poured down her legs as she discarded her choker on the table, and lined her quarter-carat diamond earrings beside it.

Jake dropped a fistful of marshmallows into both their steaming cups, and prepared to dress the third. "Jessie's not coming back," Shayla said.

"I was just making her a cup."

He was overthinking again, just like her mother used to when there'd been more month at the end of her paycheck than she could stand. *Too much responsibility,* Shayla realized, seeing her mom through grown-up eyes. "You could always eat them."

Jake lightened up, smiled. "Funny."

He delivered her cup, sat beside her, and ate one of his cookies. Jake did everything quietly. Her family would overwhelm him.

"You did a nice thing for Jessie tonight. I've never seen her so happy."

Shayla wouldn't let herself get too mushy. "She's an intelligent, highly capable woman. I think she'd make a fine doctor."

Jake shrugged. "She's never expressed an interest in medical school. She's a great nurse."

"Are you saying great nurses can't be even greater doctors?"

Jake threw up his hands. "I just said I think she's a good nurse." His eyebrows rose at Shayla's incredulous look. "And . . . if she wanted to be a doctor, she'd be a great . . .doctor. Is that better?"

"Have I ever told you you're prejudiced?"

"We covered that after basketball."

The scales tipped back, and their kiss stood between them. "You didn't listen."

Shayla wished he'd make the first move.

Instead, Jake bit into another cookie. "Wasn't planning to."

"You'd be much happier if you did, Jake."

"Don't know about that."

What was he so afraid of? She was ready for him.

His eyes slid up her elbow to her shoulder, around her neck to her chin. He was examining her, flirting in an honest, shameless way that exhilarated her.

"We collected twenty-four thousand dollars tonight."

Quietness settled around them for a moment. "You're not thirsty?" he asked.

"Is that all, Jake?"

"The money is going back."

"No, it's not."

"I run the center. I decide."

Why was he acting as if everything he said was part of some scripture? "I think the nurses are going to have something to say when they find out they're getting fired because you're stubborn and shallow and prejudiced and a close-minded man."

"You have a moustache."

Shayla threw up her hands in frustration. "You make me want to shake you until good sense seeps into that thick head of yours!"

Jake said nothing, just offered a small smile. Shayla just shook her head. "What document was Kris telling me you should reread?"

He shrugged. "The deed to this property, I believe. King says the state owns it, I say I do."

"Do you know for sure?" She flexed her aching hands.

"Yes. No." His brow knit and her heartstrings tugged. "I don't know what to believe anymore. I'll check."

"Jake, do you even have an attorney?"

He drank his cocoa and looked out into the night. "No. Haven't needed one. My grandfather's attorney, I suppose."

Shayla knew Jake saw her frustration, but she couldn't stay mad at him. Alberta and its simplicity were what Jake was about. He just didn't know the possibilities of dreaming.

"You didn't thank me," she said softly.

Jake's thumb caressed her foamy moustache away. "Who are you, Doctor Shayla Crawford?" Subtly he shifted, his warm brown gaze intent on solving her mystery.

"Who do you think I am?"

"A rich—"

She cut him off. "I'm going home."

Jake's fingers slid down her arm and she sat.

He began again. "You can't escape who you are. You're rich, Shayla. Gifted, passionate. But you're hiding something."

She bent her head at his insight. It was her turn to be quiet. And all this time, she thought he'd been avoiding her for other reasons. After his "you're rich" statement, how could she casually mention her mother was singing superstar Lauren Michaels?

Could she drag him through her extensive family tree without Jake getting caught on the Crawford family branches?

Even she had a hard time remembering all thirty-three of her cousins and their children's names.

Shayla imagined herself saying, *Jake, this is my grandfather, he was just appointed to the court of appeals. My uncles are Julian and Michael Crawford, and they just settled a billion-dollar lawsuit against a major bottling company. Why yes, that is my mother, Lauren Michaels, yes, the very one. International singing diva. Mmm-hmm. My father, of course,*

Doctor Eric Crawford. Yes, he was Mr. January in a calendar several years ago, but the family tries not to think about it. "I like to keep my skeletons where they belong," she heard herself say.

"Not fair. You've seen my life, but the window around you is very small and closed. Why?"

"You've seen my degrees and every other piece of paper that made it possible for me to be here. Who do you think I am?"

"Real, like these diamonds."

"I am real. I have a mother, and father, and a little brother. I have grandparents, and uncles, and aunts, and cousins, lots of them. I have friends and Jessie and Dee and . . . you." She twisted closer. "What did you think about our last kiss?" she asked him.

Jake didn't say a word.

"Ooh, you're bad for my ego."

"I haven't stopped thinking about it."

A tingle began at the base of Shayla's spine. "That's good news."

"Why?"

"Because I've been wanting to climb into your lap all night."

Jake didn't say a word.

She stood and the lavender silk spilled around her legs.

Shayla knew Jake now. Months of doing nothing but watching him had taught her things she wouldn't otherwise have taken the time to see.

Like his expressive eyes, crisp darkness against a bed of white satin that grew acute with his thoughts. He wanted her, possibly more than she wanted him. He had this habit of drawing in his lower lip, then releasing it moist. Jake was driving her crazy. She wanted his mouth, his damp lips, and the strength of his body against hers.

She ran her hand along his shoulders. "May I?"

Jake planted his feet and pushed the chair back.

Shayla straddled him in one fluid motion.

His eyes moved up the length of her bare legs slowly, savoring the pleasure of her weight and, for her, the first step of success.

His hands fit snugly around her calves and he used a firm grasp that got her attention and sparked her libido. Deliberately he slid them up.

Shayla breathed in and out, her toes leaving the floor as she sank into him a bit more.

By the time his hands made the trek from her calves to her butt, Shayla's breath was coming in short huffs.

On their own volition, her hands roamed his chest and neck and face and hair, until she couldn't bear the short distance between them. Their chests touched, as his hands drove sensuality into a new realm.

Rain pattered against the rooftop, the bald a cappella drumbeat native. It stimulated her blood, and by intuition her body caught a rhythm. Broken by gasps and his moans, no words were necessary.

By accident, his hands discovered the spot behind her knees, and when he touched it she jumped just enough to bring herself flush with his arousal. A long moan slithered through her body, tossing her desire into a fevered pitch.

Shayla sought the top rungs of the chair as her anchor and wanted nothing between them, not clothes, and not secrets.

Her breasts hurt, the strain to be soothed, urgent. She tipped her head to kiss him, but he pressed his arousal against her and her head fell back.

"Comfortable?" he asked, his pace steady.

"Yes, but not nearly satisfied."

"I'll see what I can do about that."

Jake drew his fingers down her collarbone, and the bumping of his hips increased. Shayla's body soared toward a climax and she told him what she wanted. "Touch my breasts."

His fingers found her C cups and he popped her left nipple into his mouth. Her sweet soprano joined the roar of the waterfall in her ears. Jake's mouth played tricks she didn't know were possible and his finger slipped beneath her dress.

Her heart beat faster. "Kiss me."

Just the thought of him tasting her sent Shayla to the door of ecstasy. Her body begged and she heard the word fall from her lips. "Please."

Jake looked up and his eyes told her what she didn't want to hear. Had she had better control of her senses, she'd have told him where he could go. But she was Jake's captive. To be dealt with as he pleased.

She closed her eyes, her body in sync with him.

When his fingers sought the sensitive tip of her womanly cove, tickles ran through her body and she went rigid.

Shayla couldn't bear knowing what he'd done. She closed her eyes so she couldn't watch him watch her explode.

Seventeen

Superhuman strength kept Jake from kissing Shayla.

If their mouths met, mountains would move, raging seas would quiet, and love would possess every molecule in his body.

The uncertainty in her eyes when she'd asked for a kiss had nearly broken his resolve, but like the fluctuating Dow, he rallied.

And now Shayla lay spent in his arms.

Her heartbeat pounded against his chest. To Jake, it was the sexiest feeling in the world. He wanted to say something, anything, but words failed him.

Shayla shifted and his feet automatically widened. Jake immediately regretted the motion. While he'd given Shayla the ultimate pleasure, his need for completion had taken a backseat and now his sex remained coiled tight against her center.

Her mouth was an inch away from his neck. Jake had never known himself to be so sensitive, but the longer

Shayla stayed against him, the more he wanted to finish what he'd started.

Her hips rotated and her legs gripped him. The tiny movement sent a king-size ripple through his body.

She looked at him. "Kiss me and I'll get up."

His brain couldn't decide, and the longer it took, the further he traveled in Shayla's ocean without a sail. He wanted to make her understand, but holding her hips transferred into helping them, and he knew he was already lost.

The tip of her tongue beckoned him as her hands closed around his neck. "Kiss me, Jake."

"Shayla. Baby, I can't."

Jake caught her hips the second she landed with purpose on top of his erection.

The heat of her breath caressed his mouth and he looked up.

Her hips shot forward and he bucked like an out-of-control adolescent, in the arms of a woman whose only purpose was to give him pleasure.

Shayla's eyes glimmered, but then she grazed his cheek, and his mouth turned to seek hers.

She moved her head and sank her teeth into his neck.

Jake's body lit up like a billion stars in the sky, and he got caught in the explosion. He rocketed into another world where her body commanded his. The chair tipped back on two legs as every muscle in his body strained to release every single shudder of desire within him. His cry of completion echoed in the quiet and he grabbed her to him so tightly, they became one, if only in one way.

Shayla stayed in his arms, tight against his chest, her creamy soft breast against his cheek. Minutes passed before the room stopped spinning and the patter of rain replaced the waves of pleasure from her breathing.

Shayla sighed, a sound so alluring, his sex wanted to respond, but needed recovery time.

"Why won't you kiss me?"

The question was so simple, yet as complex as acid rain.

"I can't give you what you deserve."

"Apparently you did." Her gaze flickered to the wet spot on his pants.

The sarcasm stung, but it was no less than what he had coming. Shayla tried to stand, but Jake couldn't let her go.

"I can't give you better than this simple log cabin and a five-year-old truck."

"It's always about you, right, Jake? I hope you enjoyed yourself."

A knock at the door startled them.

"I'll get it on my way out." Shayla stood on unsteady feet, her dress wrinkled, her body barely able to coordinate, her feelings on the bottom of Jake's shoe.

She didn't seem to care that there'd been a flood warning. She was getting the hell out of there.

"It's the middle of the night." Jake tucked her behind him. "I've got it."

Jake opened the door and took an involuntary step back. "There aren't any drugs here."

"Better not be," the woman said. "We're here for Shayla Crawford."

The man looked like he belonged in the military with his crew cut and rigid stance. The woman was tall, her hair slicked down by the rain, her hand on her holstered pistol.

Shayla took tentative steps forward. "Oh, my goodness, what are you doing here?"

A low growl rumbled through the air and both the man and the woman pulled their weapons. Jake flipped on the outside lights and they all watched the black bear disappear into the woods.

"What's going on?" Jake demanded. "Who are these people?"

"They're harmless. Come in. Come in," Shayla said to the serious couple. They hardly looked as harmless as she claimed, especially with loaded and drawn guns. "This is my aunt and uncle. Come in here."

Jake didn't know what to do besides step aside and yank his shirttail from his pants to conceal the remnants of his pleasure.

"Doctor Jake Parker," he said to the observant and very quiet couple. Shayla's family resemblance was in favor of the man.

"I'm Jade Houston-Crawford and this is my husband Nick."

"Pleasure." Jake didn't know what else to say, but their timing was remarkable, especially since he'd just compromised their niece.

"What's wrong? Is Mom or Dad sick? Has someone been hurt?" Shayla whispered. "It's Damon, isn't it?"

Nick reached out to steady Shayla, but she smacked his hand and he drew it back quickly. Jake took an unconscious step closer to Shayla's side. Something was definitely wrong.

"I told you not to touch her," Jade whispered.

"Why are you here in the middle of the night?" Shayla demanded. "Something's happened. What is it?"

"Your Grandmother Chaney has had a heart attack."

Shayla's hands flew to her forehead and she looked around as if searching for something familiar. "Where's Mom? Why didn't she call me?"

"Honey," Jade said, "she knew you had an important function tonight and she didn't want you to come home and worry."

Nick and Jade exchanged a look.

Jake recognized what transpired between them, as did Shayla. Doctors grew accustomed to controlling their emotions when delivering bad news, but for family, there was no buffer zone of protection. "She's not dead, is she?"

"No, sweetie. We need to get you home, though."

"Okay."

The searing cut of grief that etched Shayla's face would be there for life. These marks would only appear when she was afraid and unable to do more than worry. The older the person, the deeper the lines.

Jake had had them three times in his life. He reached out to Shayla but she moved toward her aunt.

She didn't want him. "Nick," Jake said, "if you'll come with me, we can get some supplies." Jake left the two women arm in arm by the window. "Where did you park?"

"Major Spears is an old friend. We borrowed his car. Tried the shortcut he told us about, but got stuck a mile back in the mudflats. My Cessna is at the airfield."

Jake grabbed ponchos, flashlights, helmets, keys, and his rifle. He gave Nick a poncho and handed one to Jade. She pulled it quickly over her head and took the other light while he slipped his on.

"The major's a good man," Jake agreed. "The rain's let up, for the moment," he said to the quiet group. "If you came through the woods, the roads are flooded."

"How will we get out, Jake?"

Jake took his suit coat and slid it onto Shayla's arms. She didn't know how much royalty flowed through her veins. She accepted the overture as if it were expected. Only he couldn't be angry, as her mind was a million miles away.

The poncho went on and Shayla took her bag from his hands.

"We'll have to take the ATVs," he said.

"Jake, my family can't ride on one of those things. We have to do something else."

"Shayla, baby," her uncle said. "Jake knows best. We'll make it."

"Okay."

Trust swept through her eyes and she turned to Jake and pulled the rifle over her shoulder. The lime-green scarf was still tied to the muzzle and handle, but Jake gave Nick an almost imperceptible shake of his head.

Some things just couldn't be explained. He herded them to the door and at Jade's insistence, let her and Nick secure the perimeter.

"We need to get to the airfield by 0220, or we won't be able to fly out until morning." The unspoken words from Nick hung in the air. Shayla's grandmother might not make it until the morning.

"It'll be a bumpy ride, but we should make it."

Jake grabbed Shayla's hands and led her out of his house and to the back of the center. She strapped on her helmet and climbed on, saying nothing. She was no longer a doctor able to deal with sickness and the possibility of death. She'd become a casualty to the cycle of life.

Jade and Nick moved efficiently, as if riding all-terrain vehicles were part of their everyday lives. They cast cautious looks at Shayla, weighing her fragility.

Jake climbed on, and Shayla wrapped her arms around his waist. She turned her head sideways, and he could feel her chest quiver, as she cried silent tears.

"We're moving north 8.6 miles, then west another three. This is a little longer, but the tree cover has hopefully protected the ground, so navigating will be easier. You okay with that thing?"

"Affirmative." Nick patted the bike. "Never met a vehicle I couldn't master. I'll take the rear."

Jake flicked on the headlights, and prayed Shayla got to her grandmother before it was too late.

Eighteen

Shayla sat behind Jake unable to stifle her grief.

In a part of her mind, she'd known the day would come when one of her relatives might become sick or even die, but she'd never imagined not having Chaney in her life. Her grandmother wasn't immortal, but part of the old life, before the Crawfords descended upon them and everything changed.

Shayla remembered sitting around her grandmother's three-sleeved dining room table, sipping hot lemonade and clipping coupons from the Sunday paper.

Every afternoon when the bus had dropped off other latchkey children, Chaney had greeted Shayla with cookies and milk, ready to hear about Shayla's day. Chaney had also been to every Little League baseball game. She'd cheer so loud, other parents would give her disapproving looks.

But Shayla had never been ashamed. She knew she was lucky.

Shayla couldn't imagine being any place right now, other than by her grandmother's side.

"Please, please, please," she heard herself moaning, and tried to calm down. She needed a focal point to distract her mind, or she wouldn't be of any help to anyone.

For the briefest second, Jake's cold, wet hand touched hers and his back curved a bit. She was already flush against him, their thighs snug, her cheek on his shoulder. But she leaned in a little farther. Needed to borrow just a bit more warmth. His strength anchored her.

The engine roared in the darkness, the woods parting as they sped through. Jake knew the way. Shayla couldn't tell one tree from another. East from west. North from south. Not in the dark. Not alone.

But Jake knew.

The entire clan of Crawfords was counting on him and he didn't even have the good sense to be intimidated. God bless him, he was shouldering a weight other men had run from.

When the vehicles careened onto the slick pavement of the airfield, it seemed as if seconds instead of minutes had passed.

Nick took the lead, and headed for his plane. Jake's stomach tightened and Shayla loosened her grip as they slowed. She climbed off and unfastened her helmet.

"Can you get the vehicle back okay?" Nick asked, as he and Jade removed their helmets.

"Major Spears and I will work it out." Jake waved to the men in the control booth. "You'd better get going."

Two workers ran onto the field and moved the ATVs.

Tension swirled around them. Jake read the carefully concealed grief in Jade's eyes. They all loved the woman named Chaney. Jake wished he'd known her too. Somehow he knew he wouldn't get that chance.

"The family is deeply indebted to you. Thank you for everything," Jade said.

"My pleasure. Take care of her."

Nick shook his hand, then bounded up the stairs with his wife behind him.

"In five, Shayla," Jade told her.

Shayla held her helmet by the straps. "I don't know how long I'll be."

"Take as much time as you need." He struggled for a moment. "I wish I could be there for you."

Shayla's heartbeat spiked, and for a few seconds the pain she'd been in eased. She wanted to reach out, have him wrap his arms around her and tell her everything was going to be all right, but Jake was backing away, even as the words had barely left his mouth.

"I have what I need," Shayla heard herself say.

"Okay." Jake's acceptance hurt like it had so many times before. Shayla started up the metal staircase when she felt Jake's touch. He pressed his mouth to her hand in a fierce kiss, and in his own language, he spoke to her. He let her go, the poncho flapping around his wet pant legs.

Tears fell and she reached for him. "Thank you," she said from the bottom of her heart. "Good—"

The wind carried the word, but he gave a brief wave and jogged to the building as if he didn't want the wind to bring him her parting words.

Shayla brought her hand to her side and stepped into the small cabin. Jade handed her a tissue. She wiped her eyes as the door was secured, and didn't look out again until she arrived home.

Chaney lay against the white sheets, ashen and frail. Tubes crisscrossed in and out of her arms. She'd been removed from the respirator. Tonight she would die. They all knew.

Shayla sat beside her grandmother's bed and held her purse. She'd been holding her grandmother's purse since she'd been old enough to walk into Sears. Shayla would sit on the floor of the dressing room, her grandmother's purse in her lap, and wait for Chaney to model for her.

Chaney had told her the secret to middle age was elastic pants and Naturalizer shoes, and Shayla still believed her.

She looked around for the comfortable kick-abouts her grandmother loved, and didn't see them. Then reality hit her square in the chest. Chaney hadn't come here under her own power. She'd been brought by ambulance with nothing but a bad heart, and her purse.

Shayla caressed the satiny smooth skin on the back of her grandmother's hand, careful of her IV.

"Grandma, I've got so much to tell you. You'd be so proud of how I've grown up. I work in a decent place. I've met so many nice people like Jessie, and Rosalie and Dee and Jake." She sighed and fished in her grandmother's purse for a peppermint. She popped it into her mouth and sheltered it in her cheek.

"You'd like him, Grandma. He's responsible, and good for me, and handsome. You'd be so proud."

A sob tore through her chest and Shayla laid her head next to her grandmother's hand. She tried to regain control of herself, but nothing could stop the tears, until fingers caressed her hair.

Shayla looked into her grandmother's wise but weak eyes.

Chaney inhaled as deep as her chest would allow and grabbed her granddaughter's hand, then caressed Shayla's cheek.

Shayla remembered falling off her bike.

Her grandmother's hands had comforted her.

Shayla had cut herself with a carving knife.

Her grandmother's hands had held her through fifteen stitches.

Shayla had moved to Alberta, Mississippi.

Chaney had folded those very same hands and prayed for her.

Now Chaney wanted Shayla to stop crying.

Shayla did her best. She pressed the call button and asked for her mother. "Save your strength, Grandma. Mom's on the way. We love you," she blurted, her eyes misting again.

Her grandmother's eyes filled with tears as they conveyed their love, then drifted closed in sleep.

The door opened and a gentle hand slid around Shayla's shoulders. She'd recognize her mother's touch in a dark room.

The comfort was immediate as Shayla slid into her mother's arms. "Mom." Shayla took her time. "She was awake for a while. I assured her of our love."

The ravages of the twenty-four-hour vigil had darkened her mother's usually glowing skin to paper-bag brown. Tiny lines streaked her bare mouth. Every once in a while, her mother would sweep her fingers across her forehead, from habit more than necessity. Two months ago, Damon had cut her bangs to tiny spikes while she napped.

Shayla let her mother sit, and pulled up the other chair.

One hour slipped into the next and her grandmother stayed with them.

"I remember the red tricycle Grandma insisted I have."

"I told her no," Lauren added, the memory just as

sweet to her. "She wouldn't let it go." Her mother drew in a deep breath. "But we have to let her go." Lauren took Chaney's and Shayla's hands in hers. "Rest, peacefully, Mother. With our love."

Shayla could say nothing as her mother released her grandmother from her earthly bond. She knew she was expected to wish her grandmother safe passage, but her heart was too heavy.

Shayla drew on strength she didn't know she had. "Grandma, you're in my heart and my mind forever. Blessings and love go with you, here." She exhaled, her throat contracting. "And in heaven. All my love."

As soon as the words left Shayla's mouth, her grandmother sighed in her sleep. "I'm going to see about Dad, okay?"

Quiet tears coursed down Lauren's cheeks. "He's in the private waiting room. Don't leave him alone, Shayla. He's taking this hard."

Shayla stopped in the hallway and wiped her eyes. Jake's cologne engulfed her as did momentary comfort. Their relationship had been tumultuous and guarded, but tonight had signaled a season of change. She'd loved being with Jake, loved feeling his hands on her body. Loved how he'd protected her and how he'd risked everything for her to be here.

She wished she were back in his cabin and away from this pain.

Her feelings were cowardly, she knew, but she was new at the grown-up game. She had to be brave. But for how long?

A part of her wanted to retreat into the spoiled overgrown child she'd been for the past eight years, but another part of her yearned to discover the strength of the real woman that lived beneath her skin. She entered the glass-enclosed waiting room and all of her uncles stood.

Nick, Justin, Michael, Edwin, Julian, and her father. She greeted each one with a kiss and hug, and ended in her dad's arms. She found real comfort there as he just rocked her.

"Dad, we gave her safe passage," she cried.

He held her tight. "It's in God's hands."

The television had been muted as the men helplessly watched Shayla and her father grieve. "Come on, sit down."

Julian, the patriarch in his father's absence, guided the couple to chairs. He stuffed their hands with tissue and prayed with them.

Her heart lightened as the uncles joined the group and spoke of uncloudy days, a pain-free life, and streets paved in gold. Shayla envisioned Chaney with black hair and her beautiful face free of lines, in heaven where elastic pants didn't matter anymore.

The weight of grief shifted and Shayla whispered, "Amen."

She sat beside her father and fit her hands snugly into his. The TV sound was turned up, and for a while they all watched the continued war in Afghanistan until the commercial, and then by silent agreement switched to *Nick at Night*.

"You look nice," her father teased.

Shayla's stomach jumped. Mud was splattered up her dress to her knees, her shoes trashed long ago. She wore footies, supplied by one of the nurses. "This is all the rage in Mississippi."

Jake's jacket offered familiarity and comfort, two

things she'd always felt when she was with him. What it lacked was what he couldn't offer. Security.

Eric considered her for a moment. "I know what the dress looked like before the mud, but the jacket is new."

What could she say to her father, a man she adored and who had changed her life as soon as he knew she was his? She still sought her father's approval. In a way, wanting to make up for all the experiences they'd never shared. "It's Jake's."

Eric Crawford, the man, missed nothing. "Jake's."

"Yes, sir." She met his gaze for a short time. "He's a good man. A good doctor. A fine person."

Her father's lips poked out as he considered her words.

"I hear it's pretty rural."

"It is."

"You ride around on three-wheelers."

"Only when we have to go into the mountains or to the airfield. Jake got us there right on time or we wouldn't be here."

"So it is very, *very quaint.*"

"We do good work. Important work." Her father leaned his elbows on his knees and she adopted the same pose. "I know you're wondering if sending me there was the right decision."

"Damn right."

"Dad, I'm a good doctor."

"I know. That's why Rodney and I can't wait for you to come back and join the practice. The new offices are incredible. We upgraded you."

"Really?" Shayla hadn't thought of the office and the practice in a long time. All she really missed besides her family was the ER, the hustle, and the adrenaline high, but not her father's OB-GYN practice, soon-to-be family practice. It sounded so mundane.

"Why'd you upgrade me?" Shayla's heart knocked against her ribs. She felt pressure in her chest, and her father's voice faded for a few seconds.

"Doesn't that sound great?" Eric asked.

"The best. Wow. It's been so long since I thought of—" Her father gave her a strange look. "What my office would look like. What's the color scheme?"

"Oh, uh—" her father stammered.

Uncle Mike joined them. "You can say April's name without me trippin'. She picked red and cream, and a huge fish tank, and some kind of art deco crap on the desk."

Shayla sat back stunned.

"Kidding," Mike said.

Shayla's mouth fell open.

Eric nudged his daughter. "He thinks he's the next Sinbad because Terra laughs at all his stupid jokes."

Shayla giggled at the metamorphosis her solid and serious uncle had made. He seemed happy and stress free. "Still on hiatus from practicing law?"

"Part-time. When I feel like it."

"He's a bum now that Terra manages that ritzy property. No mortgage, no overhead. He's a disgrace," Eric said of his older brother.

"He's jealous." Michael dismissed him. "I just took on a case you'll hear about in the news soon. High-profile CEO and a battle between the wife and mistress."

"Good for you," Shayla said, when her thoughts snapped back to the conversation she'd had with Jake. "A friend of mine may be facing a dispute with the state of Mississippi."

"What's the situation?"

"He's owned the land since his grandfather passed away, and now the state of Mississippi says the land is theirs."

"How good a friend is this?"

Good enough to climax with. "Very good." Shayla's voice caught and her father and uncle exchanged a look.

Mike touched her arm. "Tell him to fax the papers over and I'll take a look at them, as a favor to you."

"Thanks, Uncle Mike."

Keisha walked in, her black sweat suit announcing *Black Belt* in large white letters, followed by Jade, who bee-lined for Nick and gave him a dizzying kiss.

Shayla loved to see Nick thrust out of his element by his daring and sexy wife. Desire sparkled in his eyes, and Shayla saw her own maturity. She felt as if she'd found her place at the adult table.

Jade left Nick's lips long enough to hug Shayla close.

Eric interrupted the two women. "Since the cavalry is here, I'm going to sit with your mother."

"Dad, she's worried about you."

He looked at her tenderly. "If you need me—"

"Go to Lauren, Eric," Jade said as she guided him to the door. "Shayla's in good hands."

Jade had a tear in her eye when she sat beside Shayla, but it didn't fall. She was remarkably strong. "I brought you some clothes. Your dress is cute, but—"

"I know. It would look better if I added more twigs, a couple more leaves, and three or four more rips." Shayla reached for the bag, but hesitated. "I don't know. Mom might need me."

"Honey, you might as well get comfortable. Keisha and I'll stand as lookout. If anything happens, you'll be the first to know."

"Okay." Shayla couldn't help the tears that welled in her eyes. Everyone in the room was a Crawford, connected somehow or another to her father. But the day he'd accepted Shayla as his child, the entire family had adopted Lauren and Chaney, too.

They were all one big loving family.

In the bathroom, she was halfway out of the dress when the computerized voice said, "Code blue. Code blue."

Nineteen

Shayla and Lauren took turns kissing the yellow rose. Together they tossed it on top of the mahogany casket as the minister completed the service.

Chaney Wilona Slocomb had passed away quietly, her daughter and son-in-law at her side.

The family assembled back at her parents' house on Magnolia Drive, hundreds of guests milling throughout the magnificent mansion.

Shayla's aunts and cousins had taken over as hostesses, leaving Shayla and her mother time to spend with their guests. But Shayla didn't have her mother's soothing charm and open spirit.

She was tired of being nice and making small talk. Tired of walking around, trying to be brave. She just wanted to be alone to cry and soothe her aching heart.

Slipping into the long hallway, she moved on tiptoe until she reached her mother's office. There, she slipped off her shoes. Silk stockings whispered as she slid onto the chaise longue and put up her feet.

Her body ached, and her heart felt as if it were weighed down by a boulder. Shayla still hadn't found peace. Just as she closed her eyes, her cousin Tracey stuck her head in the office. "Shay?"

"How did you find me?"

"I saw you slip out. Jake Parker on line one."

"He is?" She sat up, her feet searching for her shoes.

"For only the tenth time in three days."

Shayla hobbled when the shoes didn't go on all the way. "Why didn't someone tell me?"

"Your grandmother just died. We didn't think you wanted to talk."

"I would have talked to him," she protested.

Tracey's eyes saddened. "You just looked like you wanted to have some time alone."

Shayla picked up the phone. "Thanks, Tracey."

"Doctor Parker sounds cute. A little country, but sexy."

Shayla narrowed her eyes. "If you don't get out, I'll tell your father you had sex when you were fifteen."

"You're evil," Tracey said and shut the door.

Shayla exhaled slowly. She put the phone to her ear and pressed the line. "Hello?"

"Hey, Shayla." Jake sounded surprised. "I didn't think I'd get to speak to you."

Immediately she was taken back to the sweet smell of pine after the rain, and the peaceful quiet of her cabin. "How are you, Jake?"

"Fine. You?" The background noise of the center faded.

"Okay," she lied. "Not really. Hard, you know?" Shayla said as few words as possible. She couldn't yet speak of her grandmother in wistful terms. Shayla still expected to hear Chaney's laughter or see her glasses perched on the end of her proud nose.

But Jake had already seen her cry. He'd felt the first trembles of her fear. He'd been the first to say he was sorry. That mattered to her.

"I know it's hard." Jake's voice touched her aching heart.

"I—" they said together.

"Go ahead," Shayla told him.

Back at Jake's cabin, they'd shared something special and she wanted to explore the possibilities. Although she felt grown up, she wished she didn't have to hurdle obstacles to find that easy air of loving contentment Nick and Jade shared.

Or the gooey love that Terra and Mike had. Or the passion her mother and father shared. Or even the solid love that bound Julian and Keisha.

"Can I come see you?"

"No." Shayla covered her face. "I didn't mean that."

She twirled the Imperial Clover Faberge egg her father had given her mother for Christmas last year. Shayla lifted the lid and the enamel hummingbird began to rotate to the strains of "Waltz of Flowers" by Tchaikovsky.

She'd loved this house since her parents built it five years ago, but for the past seven months, she'd discovered the pleasure of simple living.

"What do you mean, then?"

"I just mean I can't handle our differences yet. I'm under too much pressure right now."

"You're listening to classical music?"

Shayla gingerly lowered the lid. "Not really. I was just goofing around with the remote," she lied again, knowing she was right to evade Jake.

"You don't want to see me, Shayla?"

She felt his lips against her hand again. Felt the strength from his body and how he'd held her suspended on the wooden legs of the chair. He offered a comfort she'd never known with a man, and his voice nudged her closer to changing her mind.

But could he understand all this? The wealth, the glamour, and the family?

One day her double life was going to blow up in her face. Just not right now. She couldn't handle it. "I don't want you to come here because I'm coming back tomorrow."

"Are you sure, Shayla?" Jake sounded worried. "It's only been a week. The service was today—I wasn't trying to rush you."

"I know." Shayla felt as if she were the broken pieces of a jigsaw puzzle that had been scattered by a reckless child. Her senses told her to tread cautiously. "What's the situation with your land, Jake?"

"Hey," he said softly. "Don't worry about it right now. I took everything to an attorney and we're sorting it out."

"That's good. I was just concerned," she rattled on. "My uncle is an attorney."

"Wow. Marine Corps officers, gun-toting aunt, and an attorney."

"Jade's a bounty hunter."

"Any supreme court judges?" he teased.

Shayla laughed. "No." The word was out and she counted three times in one conversation that she'd lied to Jake. Shayla didn't even try to justify herself. She just didn't want to feel his rejection. Not today when she needed someone to care about her feelings. "My uncle has offered to look over your papers. For free. You know. As a favor."

"Is he with a big firm?"

"No. He works out of his home. You know the saying, two eyes are better than one."

Jake paused. "I guess I know when I need help. *Somebody* has done a good job teaching me that."

"Why not?" Jake said. "I'll mail them."

"Or—" she suggested, knowing if she didn't push, he would try to appease her. A week ago, they'd have argued about her interference, but not now. Jake, and everyone, was treating her with kid gloves. Shayla didn't feel human anymore. Just weak and sad. "You could fax them and he'd get them right away. Here's the number. Got a pen?"

"Sure. Go."

Shayla rattled it off. "Everybody there okay?"

"Yep. Worried about you."

"What?" That surprise brought her to tears. She sniffed and wiped her eyes. "I need to dry up the waterworks."

"Why, Shayla?"

"Because I'm too old for this." She cleared her throat.

"I think it's too soon for you to come back."

"Jake Parker, I've never known you to be so protective." Shayla leaned into the sound of his voice.

"Shayla Crawford is a stubborn woman, and sometimes she needs someone to be protective of her."

"Oh, really?"

"Definitely."

"Do you need anything?" she asked softly.

"Huh?"

Some of her pain eased. "I can't believe the great Doctor Parker just said 'huh.' "

Their chuckles faded until there was just the sound of their breathing. "I'm selfish. I know this isn't politically correct, but I want you to come back," he said. Shayla wanted to float away and catch a southwesterly wind back to his arms. "Although I wish you'd let me come to you."

Shayla's gaze slid to the platinum records that were mounted on the walls of her mother's office. It wasn't just the accoutrements of success and wealth, but her mother was *Lauren Michaels.*

The door opened and her cousin Trisha stuck her head in. "Amy and her father just arrived."

"I'll be right there."

"Okay." Trisha waved and ducked out.

"I wish you meant that," he said.

"What?"

"That you'd be right here."

"Jake," she whispered his name.

"Shayla."

His voice caressed her and Shayla wondered how long it'd take to pack. She needed to stop by a candle store. Jessie might like a pair of the earrings she was so fond of admiring from Shayla's jewelry box. And Dee could use an oscillating fan.

"I can't come back to the same situation. If you can't kiss me, and love me the way I want to be loved, I don't know where this can go."

Background noise faded, and his voice practically caressed her ear. "I know you'll break my heart."

Shayla clutched her chest as the words threw her into shock. She'd never heard a man speak so intimately, so honestly. "Why would I do that?"

"You just would, baby."

Rivulets of desire spread through her like rain on dry land.

"Doctor Parker?" Dee said, stealing seconds from their intimate moment.

Shayla dropped her head as Jake gave fast instructions. "We've got a full house," Dee reminded him.

"Another two minutes and I'm on my way," he said. "Shayla."

"You have two minutes, Doctor Parker, and I'm not going to let you off that easy. Admit how you feel about me."

"I like you."

"A lot?" she asked.

"Yes, a lot."

"How much is a lot?" she asked, pushing for more.

"A whole lot."

Her body began to tingle. "You think I'm pretty?"

"Stunning." They were definitely getting somewhere. "You like me, too." He turned the tables on her.

"I wouldn't have been bouncing around in your lap if I didn't." Shayla adopted her mother's habit of sitting on her foot, the other swinging.

His low growl tickled her center. "I'd better go," he said.

"You're such a baby," she teased, hoping he'd take the bait.

"Babies don't feel the way I felt the other night."

"How'd you feel, Jake?"

"Come on," he hedged. "Let me go back to work."

"You wanted to make love to me."

His breath caught. "Yes," he said in a low measured tone. "I wanted to make love to you."

"Then why didn't you?"

"You know why."

"I don't get you for one minute."

"What don't you get? That I'm falling in love with you? That I know if I kiss you again, I'll be lost forever?" His voice deepened. "You're going to leave here in a couple months and I'll be alone again. That's what I think about, Shayla."

Shayla saw it all. His resistance to her, his reluctant

acceptance of her ways and habits and the changes she'd made. She'd stolen his world and made it her own. And soon she'd leave. "I don't know what to say."

"I didn't tell you so you could do something. Life is as it is, Shayla. We can't miss our moments. Then life is nothing. Right?"

"We need you up here *working*," Pearline said to Jake with censure in her voice.

She must have surprised him, because all Shayla heard was his muffled voice for a few seconds. "One minute."

"Jake—"

"Pearline, I said give me a minute!" Jake returned to the phone. "She's driving me crazy. Either she's bipolar or just nuts."

"If you find me difficult, imagine what she thinks."

"Don't tell me you're siding with her."

"No, Jake. I just understand her. I don't like her ways or her attitude, but I certainly know how I affect people. Anyway," she said, rubbing her eyes, "you're tired. I can hear it in your voice. I'll be back tomorrow. Bye, Jake." Shayla hung up and took the narrow staircase off her mother's office to the third floor.

In her room, she went into her twenty-foot-deep closet and selected from the row of neatly pressed pants. She changed into a bright top. She needed the color to help raise her spirits. So as not to seem disrespectful, Shayla added a black jacket and two-inch heels.

Downstairs, Shayla visited with Amy and her father, saw them off, and ended up in the kitchen.

Aunts Keisha, Ann, and Cheryl moved food from pans and pots to plates and platters. There was enough to feed an army.

She leaned into her brother's playroom off the kitchen. "Skooch?"

Damon zoomed over to her. He never walked anywhere. And he was sure he could fly. She caught him in midair. "You crazy little thing. You can't fly." She kissed him until he giggled.

Finally he grabbed her face and she looked into incredible gray eyes. "Yes, I can!"

"Madman," her six-year-old cousin Phillip called. "It's your turn." Damon scrambled down from Shayla and zoomed back to play video games.

Shayla stepped back into the kitchen. "Need any help?" she asked Cheryl, who scooped smothered meatballs out of a Crock-Pot.

"Honey, you could gain some weight. You and your mother really shouldn't disrespect the fat women in the family by staying so thin."

"Speak for yourself," Ann said. "I'm not fat. I'm pleasantly round."

Her aunts giggled. "Men want something to hang on to, is that it?" Keisha asked, six-two, and one hundred eighty pounds of muscle.

"Shut up. You're out of the club." Cheryl used her butt to move Keisha aside. "Goodness, this trash is everywhere."

"I'll get it." Shayla gathered the bags and stepped out the back door. She dumped the trash, strolled back inside, and stopped short.

All her aunts were staring at her. "What the hell is going on in Mississippi?" Cheryl demanded.

"Somebody stole Shayla and sent back this impostor."

Ann wiped Shayla's hands with a cloth filled with soapy water.

Cheryl felt her forehead. "You've never taken out the trash. *Ever.* What are they doing to you?"

Shayla drew her hands back and grasped a paper towel. "Nothing. We take turns taking out the trash."

"Your father doesn't know about this," Keisha insisted. "Or else he'd put a stop to it right now."

"What kind of facility makes the doctors take out the trash?" Cheryl demanded.

"Sounds like a hellhole to me," Ann announced.

Shayla backed toward the dining room. "It's really okay. Don't worry."

A plate of sandwiches sat on the counter and she picked one up. "See, I'm eating."

She popped the bread into her mouth and started chewing, then stuck out her tongue, scraping it with a napkin. "Ick!"

"You didn't see that big piece of cucumber? This *is* our Shayla," Keisha told the other women. "For a minute I thought you were an alien. False alarm."

Lauren walked in as the talk resumed. As her mother strolled through, her sisters-in-law reached out and stroked her or gave her hugs. Shayla felt their love.

"Sweetheart, can I see you for a minute?" her mother asked.

"Sure." She quickly fixed the plastic bag in the can and dropped in her napkin. She washed her hands and followed her mother to her office.

Inside, her father waited.

"What's up?" she asked them.

Lauren walked over to her desk and picked up a packet of papers. Shayla hadn't noticed them when she'd been at her mother's desk, but as her mother approached, the anxiety returned.

"These are for you from your grandmother. Mom lived a long life and she was a very wise woman." Lauren struggled to keep her voice steady.

As Shayla expected, her father went to her mother's side and rubbed her back. "I worked most of my life as a financial planner, and it seems my mother was a better investor than I.''

"What are you saying, Mom?"

"Your grandmother started a college fund for you long ago, but when your dad stepped in and paid for college, I guess she just rolled it over and made even more investments—'' Her mother sucked in air and closed her mouth.

Heat flashed through Shayla. "How much money are we talking about?" she whispered.

"A lot."

Shayla's head felt as if snare drums were inside. "A lot" was not a term ex-financial planners used. They dealt only in finite numbers. Suddenly, Shayla stood.

The content of the envelope was going to change her life.

Shayla's first thought was relief, followed closely by the tug-of-war between love and acceptance of love lost. She didn't want to look back over her life and wonder about the things she hadn't pursued. The feelings she had for Jake were the blush of first love. She had to see where this road ended. "I'm going back to work." Shayla walked away from her parents. "Today."

"I don't understand." Fear in her mother's voice made Shayla turn. "Your grandmother left you a great deal of money."

"I can't deal with this right now."

"Honey, your grandmother worked all her life and now a part of the result of her effort is yours."

"Mom, I'm not rejecting Grandma. I just can't handle another thing right now." A sob broke from her. "I'm too emotional. It's too much."

"Shayla, sweetheart, you can't hide from your inheritance," her father said.

"I need time." She was at the door, her back to her

parents. "Let me go back to work. I'll call in a few weeks. We can talk then. I promise."

Her father reached her first, then her mother. "Are you sure?" her dad said.

"I'm positive. Let me go, okay?"

"Okay."

They stepped back and Shayla quickly looked away from their teary eyes as she left the office. In her room, she threw clothes into new suitcases, her mind reeling. All her life she'd wanted to be rich and now her grandmother had made that dream come true.

Even if it were only ten thousand dollars, it was more than she had. But Shayla faced the first real thing she'd have earned on her own since before she'd become a Crawford.

She'd worked hard for Jake's love. And he did love her.

But not enough to stop pushing her away.

Something deep inside made Shayla reach for him in a way she'd never done for a man. She could totally get her feelings hurt. But Shayla felt the quest was worth the fight.

Shayla hugged her mother as her father and her uncles packed her father's brand-new Mercedes for her. Her family covered the driveway and lawn, each waiting to say good-bye and give her their love. She hopped into the big car and blew a kiss as she pulled away. She saw the waving clan in her rearview mirror. Their love for her was solid.

What she had with Jake could break her heart.

But Shayla had to find out.

Twenty

Jake closed the center for the night and pushed his weary feet toward home. Another fourteen-hour day, and all he could think of was Shayla and sleep. Thank God it was Saturday.

Rain slipped through the bare forest branches and glided down his skin. Too tired to shield himself, he allowed the thick drops to wash away some of his fatigue as a cold November wind shifted through the air.

Soon snow would drape Christmas tree branches, and the men who'd labored in the cotton fields all summer would suit up in insulated coveralls and cut down the winter crop.

He'd see the fallout, the severed limbs from chain saw accidents, and a few toes and fingers lost to frostbite. And then there'd be the annual five cases of alcohol poisoning. For twenty years, the church wives took a weekend winter retreat, and their husbands took that time to test limits they no longer possessed.

He'd see it all for a while. Then he, like everyone else, would have to make a decision. Go to the new hospital or stay on the wrong side of Alberta.

Jake walked slowly, the words in the deed a betrayal of everything he'd ever known. The land Jake thought he owned wasn't his any longer. Twenty years ago his grandfather had promised the government the land. Dobbs King and the rest of the Mississippi politicians were simply collecting on a promise.

Jake listened to the squish of his boots against the wet leaves and knew he was still alive. The sound was all that anchored him to land that had been in his family for nearly one hundred years.

Jake didn't feel better knowing he still owned seventy acres of the surrounding property that the lake and cabins sat on. In his mind he'd lost the most important part.

Jake trudged past a sign on a tree, HOME, the letters runny and weathered. He saw Shayla's cabin then, the cold blackness mocking him. Maybe she'd changed her mind.

He followed the direction of the runny arrow, and noticed that the lights in his cabin were on. His footsteps quickened and he prayed his intruder was tall, beautiful, and could make his heart stop at a hundred paces.

Jake took the stairs in twos and opened the door.

Shayla stood across the room, a fire starter in her hand.

"Hey," he said softly so as not to scare her.

"Hey yourself." The energy she'd come to be known for was gone. "You're all wet. I'll get a towel."

The sparkle had disappeared, stolen by the greedy claws of grief. Pounds had melted away, her pants barely hugging her hipbones.

His Shayla, the Shayla he could love and be infuriated

with at the same time, was buried beneath this scarecrow of a woman.

She came back and started rubbing his face with the towel.

"I've missed you," he said.

Her hands slowed. "How much?"

He pulled her at the waist and caught her neck in a tender kiss. Temptation taunted him, but his alter ego issued a stern warning. She was still as soft as he remembered, but not alive the way *his* Shayla had been.

Jake let her go. "Are you staying?" he asked her.

"Ask me to stay."

"Shayla, stay."

"Yes," she whispered.

Jake pressed a kiss into her palm. He threaded their fingers and guided her around the cabin extinguishing all the candles except those in the bathroom.

"We'll take a shower, okay?" She gave a nod, but said nothing. "To warm up," he added, hoping she'd fill in the quiet with her usual challenging chatter. In the bathroom, he turned on the water, and steam started to swirl around them.

Shayla stepped from her shoes. For the first time he realized they weren't heels. Never since he'd known her had Shayla worn flats. He picked up the fine-grain leather. "I don't like these."

Her eyes shifted to the garbage can where he'd thrown her shoes. She just sighed.

Fear snaked through him. He expected to get cussed out, told off, or something. Not a sigh. Not from his Shayla.

Jake turned her away from him. He pulled down the zipper on her pants, and eased her feet from the legs.

Goose bumps covered her thighs, but despite the steam, she remained cold.

He pulled her against him, his fingers hooking the waist of her high-cut panties. Jake looked at her face in the mirror and wanted to see her eyes flash just once. A flicker would mean there was life in there somewhere. But he got nothing.

Jake popped the band and drew them from her, his arm around her waist, her butt pressed into him.

Still nothing from her.

But Jake couldn't say the same thing for himself. He'd wanted nearly two weeks for her to return, but this woman wasn't the one he wanted. He wanted the passionate woman that had set his world on fire. But just like a slow-starting fire, he had to nurture her and hope the Shayla he wanted so desperately hadn't died with her grandmother.

Jake drew his hand up her stomach and slowly unhooked the satiny material and let it fall. Shayla said nothing when he helped her into the shower. All Jake could hear was the stinging pelt of water against the curtain and the swish of wind and leaves against the cabin's logs.

This wasn't right. This wasn't Shayla. Engulfed with stubborn desire, he peeled his clothes away and climbed into the shower with her.

Shayla's body was sculpted to perfection.

She grew shy under his intense gaze and he reached for the one emotion that had snuck through her haze. Jake wouldn't let her withdraw any more. He pulled her to him.

She shuddered. "I'm cold."

Water bounced off her shoulders and he turned until she faced the wall. He understood her grief. He'd stood at the bulletproof glass window of death, a spectator, unwilling to bang his head hard enough to get through.

Jake lathered his hands and pushed them into her

shoulders so hard the air shot from her lungs. He drew down her stiff shoulders and under her arms. She didn't cry, didn't move, her body pressed against the wall as if she were the victim of a stickup, but Jake continued his assault, raking his fingers over her tight bottom and down her legs. She tightened her knees. The second sign of life.

Jake forced himself to deny his own pleasure as his erection bobbed painfully but he couldn't take much more. So he bit her.

"Ooh." The moan oozed from Shayla's mouth like ice cream over hot apple pie. There was no pain involved, just the moan of pleasure.

Jake bit her thigh, then above her wet nest of curls, and then the underside of her left breast. Her hands fluttered and she cut off the water.

"Shayla," he whispered.

"I'm here, Jake." Her hands found his ribs and curved around his waist.

Jake reached past the curtain and grabbed two thick towels.

He wrapped her hair and body, and guided her to the bed, then dried himself. Jake lowered himself beside her. "I'm glad you're back."

"I'm glad you were waiting."

Jake pulled her down on top of him.

He dragged his hands up until he cupped her butt. Only then did he look at her face. Jake kissed her cheek and felt the smooth texture of her skin against his tongue.

She laughed deep in her throat and pushed her towels to the floor. "I want to hold you."

"I want to make love to you," he said.

A small smile tipped up the corners of her mouth.

"It's about time. I thought you were going to drown me."

Jake smoothed back her wet hair. He kissed her nose, her eyes, pressed his lips into her temple and her ears.

Jake wanted to touch the flames, wanted to claim her lips that beckoned with forbidden temptation.

She clung to him when his mouth covered her breast, and he wanted to give her completion the right way this time, for both of them.

Shayla's mouth grazed his nipple and he sucked in a deep breath. He shifted them sideways and her teeth continued their pleasurable assault.

Jake's hands shot through her wet hair.

"Does that feel good?" she asked as she nuzzled his chin.

"What are you doing to me?" he asked, feeling drunk.

Shayla stopped. "I don't know."

"Come here." He guided her face back. "Do that again."

Her lips closed over the tiny tip.

Jake brought her flush against him, when her body started to writhe, her reaction so much more than he expected.

When Jake's tongue left her breast and slid down her stomach, Shayla bucked in an uneven earnest tempo.

Their shadows danced against the wall and she reached for him, but Jake held her hands. "Jake, let me touch you."

"In a minute."

His tongue made her wiggle in delight, and by the time his lips covered the erect tip, Shayla spun in a dizzying climax.

When she landed and opened her eyes, Jake was smiling down at her. "There's more," he assured her.

"Oh my God."

Jake sat up and Shayla scooted back enough for him to pull the condom into place. She laced her legs behind him and waited until he'd gotten the head of his erection inside of her.

"Jake?"

"Shayla."

"It's my first time," she said, and pushed herself onto him.

Twenty-one

Shayla, a virgin?

How could that be?

She was so sexy. So confident. So enticing. So completely alluring out of bed with the roll of her hips, the way her tongue darted across her lips, her clothes, everything about her shouted, "I've had sex!"

Jake looked at her, but didn't see her. Held her, but couldn't feel her. Inhaled her scent, but couldn't distinguish her smell. The message his brain was receiving from his body didn't connect into a consistent pattern.

Shayla was a virgin.

Suddenly, Shayla had his face in her hands, forcing him to look at her. Her hips bumped his. "Hey, get in the game or get off the court."

Heat flashed through Jake's body like an unleashed stream. All of his senses registered at once. His eyes never left hers as he guided himself slowly into her.

Shayla smiled up at him. "Are you all the way in?"

Jake laughed and his member jumped. "I can't concentrate if you make me laugh."

"There'll be no laughing then," she said and opened wider for him.

"It'll hurt. Just for a minute."

"I know, sweetheart."

Jake thrust hard and absorbed her shocked squeal through his shoulder where her teeth sank. "Jake," she whispered, as he lay above her afraid to move, afraid not to.

"Shayla?"

"Make love to me." This time her husky voice filled with yearning was all he needed.

"Yes." He saw stark awareness in her eyes and strove for that glazed-over, excited flush he knew she was capable of.

"Hold me," he told her.

Shayla's hands fluttered against his slick back. "Here." Jake placed her palms against his butt. "Squeeze." He was tempting fate. Playing games with his mind and body in order to give her the most pleasure possible. Completion wasn't far away, but he had to make sure she was satisfied first. Her first time.

With any man. And she'd chosen him. Jake tried to separate his mind and body as they fell into a quick rhythm. He distracted himself by sucking on her earlobe, but this only drove Shayla into him faster.

When he looked at her again, a thin sheen of moisture covered her top lip, and the happily glazed look was almost there.

He let her guide his thrusts, her body receiving all of him.

Jake welcomed the quickening in her hips and the telltale fluttering around his organ. Her nails raked his back and her body arched into him. "Oh," she said. "Oh. Ohhh, Jake."

The tender cry of his name unlocked his release, and he leaped into bliss and soared.

Shayla lay beneath Jake, as he caught his breath. His mocha-colored skin glistened from exertion. She kept trying to convince herself this was what she wanted, but her mind tripped over the fact that she'd waited twenty-five years to finally commit herself in the ultimate act of intimacy and he wasn't even her boyfriend.

Shayla didn't believe in regrets, but she was aware that this was probably a bad mistake.

She needed to think and balance everything in private, because she was sure she was about to cry. "I have to go."

Jake swore and Shayla closed her eyes. He'd never cursed in her presence before. "No."

"Jake, I need to go." Shayla hated the weakness she heard in her own voice.

"No! No," he said more calmly. "That's not how it's done. You and I both wanted to make love. You waited twenty-five years to give your virginity to me, and I'm not going to let you ruin what we just shared. Talk to me. Cry. I don't care what you do, but I don't want you to go."

She closed her eyes and shut him out. His thumb slid down her cheek. "Look at me," he whispered.

Shayla didn't want him to see her vulnerability, but she couldn't deny wanting to hurt him until he let her go. She was angry and afraid and she knew it was all reflected in her eyes.

"Like what you see?"

"Aw, baby." He nuzzled her and whispered her name. "I could swim in their depths forever."

"That's me. Deep." This wasn't at all what she expected. She sniffed, and gripped the sheets.

"Shayla, don't act like this." He played with her still damp hair. "You're hurting my feelings."

"You're not funny."

Jake was pushing her, guiding her out of her insecurity, but to go where? He loved her but couldn't commit because he was positive she'd never be happy with him.

What would he do when he found out she had money?

"I think I'm going to cry," he said in her ear. "Do you want me to cry? Boo-hoo."

She giggled despite herself and she made a conscious effort to table her financial situation until later. "Okay. Stop. You're torturing me."

"Stay?"

She hesitated. "I'll stay."

Jake waited a moment, unable to take his eyes off her. "What just happened?"

"You want the truth?"

"I don't expect anything less from you."

Her unsteady voice broke into the quietness. "I understand why people should wait until they're married before making love."

"You're in love with me," he stated matter-of-factly.

"Right." Shayla knew she'd implied it before, but if Jake was going to dump her, she wanted to know right now.

"When?"

"Somewhere between your fifth and eighth call, last week."

Jake sighed. "I thought you were avoiding me."

"I was."

"Because you weren't going to come back?"

Shayla shook her head no.

"Then why?"

"I can't say without being embarrassed," she whispered.

"Baby, we've done it all. You can say anything to me."

"Why aren't you freaked out? Why don't you just let me walk out of here?" she demanded. She couldn't tell him he didn't love her enough because if he agreed, her heart would shatter.

"That wouldn't solve this situation."

"Now we have a situation?" She cursed beneath her breath.

"Such language from a proper woman," he admonished while tasting her neck. "Tell me."

Shayla's fingers danced along his rib cage. She could feel him getting hard again. "The things I'm thinking about are not proper."

"Then I should definitely know what they are."

She pushed him until she was on top. "You don't love me back."

Jake drew his bottom lip between his teeth, concentrating on how their bodies moved. The thrusts hurt more than her bared soul. But there was only so much she could take. Shayla moved to dismount, when Jake sat up and dragged her legs around his back.

"Be still."

"You're too much for me."

"That's not true." He slowed his thrusts and despite the fact that he'd just taken a meat cleaver to her heart, she still wanted him.

"You're too big," she said even as she sighed.

Jake bit her collarbone. "No, I'm not."

"Why does it hurt?" She sought the answer for her nether region as well as her heart.

"Loving sometimes hurts." Jake's hands had moved up to her neck. "After a while, it feels very good."

"Mmm," she said as her rise to pleasure began. He was telling the truth.

"Look, baby."

Shayla watched as the length of him stretched outside her body, then slowly disappeared. Watching their bodies meet and retreat was like putting their lovemaking to music.

Shayla caught Jake looking at her lips.

"Hurt still?" he asked.

"No," she moaned, as her body rolled into his.

Jake captured her breast in his hand, felt it completely before he brought the tip to his mouth. Her head fell back as she clasped his shoulders, no longer trying to be free of him.

"Say it," she demanded, her hips moving in determined circles. "Just say it."

Jake's gaze reflected the shift in control. She saw caution flood the smoky depths and she didn't care. They both had a lot to lose. "Say you love me."

Their bodies met again.

"Shayla."

"Tell me," she urged, her mouth moving closer to his.

She could no longer control anything about her heart or her body.

"I love you."

As he sent her toward the apocalypse, he turned her face, and sealed her mouth with a soul-stirring, climactic kiss.

Twenty-two

Shayla staggered home Sunday morning and poured herself into a lukewarm tub of jasmine-scented water.

Her body relaxed, but her mind embarked on a journey she couldn't escape. Her own shame.

Her grandmother was barely in the ground and Shayla had let her grief be the catalyst for losing her virginity. No matter how Jake tried to convince her, she'd been reckless and unfair to him.

She was Shayla Crawford. Doctor. Daughter. Friend. Grieving granddaughter.

How could she have given herself away at a time like this?

If she'd been in Atlanta, there'd have been someone to caution her against her impulsive nature. But here, there was no one to answer to but herself.

This was the growing up her father had been talking about.

She wasn't a bad person, but occasionally she made

bad decisions. Shayla pulled the plug and let the water out of the claw-footed tub, cleaning up as she went.

It was ironic, she thought as she put away the cleaning supplies, then dressed. A year ago, she'd have left her bathroom a wreck, because the housekeeper would pick up after her. But today was different.

She tried not to be too hard on herself as she brushed her hair into a wrap, then lay down with a cool cloth over her eyes. She'd matured, but not nearly enough.

The cabin was quieter than her parents' house, quieter even than Jake's, where she'd been lulled to sleep by the slap of the waves against the shore. But her cabin was farther from the lake than Jake's and all she heard was her beating heart and the wind whistling through the tiny crack in the cabin walls.

A furious knock swept the door.

"Who is it?" she called from her room.

"Me. Can I come in for a minute?"

"For what?"

"I need to talk to you."

Shayla stepped over open suitcases, and opened the door. "What is it?"

"Why the attitude?"

She crossed her arms. "If you don't know, I can't help you."

Jake closed the door and leaned against it. "I wouldn't fit in your world."

"I'm out there. Do you see me?"

"I see you," he said softly. "You're beautiful."

"That's the first time you've ever said that to me."

"You knew."

She looked into his eyes and loved him like crazy. "It's different for you. But it was my decision, my virginity."

"Shayla, it's mine, too."

"If you don't mind, I'll own up to the mistake by myself, if it's all the same to you."

"Shayla." Guilt rang in the way he called her name.

She turned away from him. "I remember your face right before you kissed me. Sadness was so deeply etched in your eyes, I reached out and tried to touch it. My hand grazed your chest. For a minute, I experienced unconditional love. You don't have to look in the window anymore. I'm inside, Jake."

His head moved in a tortured jerk. "Baby, you'd never be satisfied with me. I'd never be enough."

Even as he said the words, the physical pull between them was tremendous. Shayla defied gravity and stayed away from him.

"Was there anything else?" She sorted her clothes for the dresser and closet and put them away while he watched from the center of her living-room floor. Eventually nothing stood between them but an empty suitcase. Shayla zipped it closed and stood it up in her room against the wall.

"Trappers caught the bear."

She stopped. "What did they do with him?"

"Moved him away. He won't bother us anymore."

"Good. Anything else?"

He shrugged. "I guess not." Jake got to the door, but turned back. "You're just like them, Shayla."

"Go ahead and call out your enemy, Jake. That way I know how to defend myself. Are you talking about the rich?"

"Yes. They don't care about the poor. All they care about is themselves, their stupid museums, and preserving their wealth. The workers who keep the state running are an afterthought. Their care is left to doctors like me who sacrifice everything to make sure they have some quality to their humble lives. You want me to be something I'm not. I can't leave. Ever. This is where I belong."

"I never left, Jake, but you keep trying to pigeonhole me in order to protect yourself. I'm still here even after the hell your sister put me through."

A quiet moment passed before he spoke. "You're passing through."

Shayla got in his face. "Why is being poor such a badge of honor for you?"

"There is no honor," he exploded. "You know why you only see children? Their parents are too ashamed of their poverty and ignorance."

"That's a lie."

"Is it? I've counted. For every twenty children, you see one adult. You can paint a building and give them trinkets, but it doesn't change their lives once they go home. They're embarrassed by you, Shayla."

All of her carefully constructed control collapsed. "I was orphaned at three when my birth mother died. Foster care took me in, and I was adopted when I was four. Two years later, my adoptive father died. My mother and my grandmother and I lived on Spam and government cheese until my mother got her degree and became a financial planner. We could barely make ends meet for a long, long time. My adoptive mother and my biological father met and married eight years ago, and between them and the rest of my family, we've changed our lives. Every time I look at one of the single mothers that comes to me for care, every time I see Eliza and her baby or Rosalie and her baby, I see my mother, and I see my face in their children.

"So shut up about what I am! I'm rich because my

parents worked hard to pull themselves up. I'm rich because I'm not afraid of what's around the next corner. I'm rich because I'm strong enough to walk away from you, a man I thought had vision, but I now see is blinded by his own sight. Now get out of my house.''

Twenty-three

Shayla's words ripped Jake to shreds.

They drove inside to the core where he'd banked humility like money in an offshore account. He was as guilty as a man with the bloody DNA on his shirt.

For years he'd worn his badge of honor like a superhero emblem, and over time, people had bought into his fairy tale. Now he was *the* man. But another man was threatening, not his ability, but his purpose.

If the center wasn't here, then who was Jake Parker?

Jake stared at the man in his bathroom mirror. It was the same face, but he didn't recognize the person.

He leaned closer and what he saw so deep inside made his tongue turn salty and his heart thunder with dread.

He saw his father.

Lonny Parker. Lover. Father. Leaver.

Thirty-three years folded together, like the pages of a book.

One night his father had gone out for cigarettes and never came back. A postcard arrived within a week stating he was looking for work in Louisiana. No return address.

Five months later, another arrived still full of hope and dreams for their future, still no return address. And every few months after that, another would arrive. But then weeks slipped into months, and then months rolled into years, until the cards stopped altogether. By the third card, Jake had stopped being fooled. But his mother and sister stayed hopeful. His mother until the day she died.

His father had walked out of his life for a pack of cigarettes and no responsibility for the lesson he'd taught his son.

Jake had seduced Shayla's love, playing the "I want you, don't want you" game. He'd romanced her virginity from beneath her skirt, grabbed hold of her heart, and thrown it back in her face.

He'd played sadists' roulette as he'd done with a dozen other women, but this time he'd been bitten back. Shayla'd stuck her pointy-toed high-heeled shoe in his game, and spun the wheel in the opposite direction.

She'd told him to kiss off.

On Monday morning, Jake walked into the center and saw Shayla behind the counter, tapping away on her laptop. "Doctor Crawford," he said.

"Doctor Parker." Her newly done hair glistened as she picked up her half-eaten bologna sandwich and laptop, walked into room two, and closed the door.

On the way, Pearline and Shayla passed without speaking.

Jessie burst into the center. "Where's Doctor Crawford?"

"Holed up in room two," Pearline said. "Eating a bologna sandwich."

Jessie frowned. "Yuck. Bologna at seven in the morning? I'll go see what's up with her."

"Don't bring back any bad news," Pearline advised. "I already got a headache."

"Pearline," Jake said, "I'm warning you. Not today. One more word and you'll be sorry."

"Fine," she retorted.

Jake turned to Dee. "Make a note that the Gonzaleses are supposed to come in today. Their car broke down, so I'll have to go get them."

"Doctor Crawford already volunteered to pick them up," Dee informed him with a pleasant smile.

"Really?" Pearline walked over to the counter. "When?"

"This morning. Pearline, I am the office manager, in case you forgot."

"What's your problem?" she snapped. "Did she bring back some of her high-and-mighty attitude and give it to you?"

"Pearline," Dee hissed. "Shut your mouth! Her grandmother just passed. I didn't used to care for Doctor Crawford, but a long time ago I realized she isn't the enemy. All she's done is help us, and all you've done is be cruel and vindictive. If I was really in charge of this office, I'd fire your bitter behind so fast your head would spin—Oh, goodness, forgive me." Dee's eyes were locked over Pearline's shoulder.

Shayla faced Jake's sister, the straw broom in her hand.

"You've been dying to say something to me; here's your chance."

Pearline put her hand on her hip. "If you want to know the truth, I don't like you."

"Now there's a secret. Tell me something I don't know."

"You came in here like you own the place. All you did was change things and take over. And now you've turned friend against friend. None of this was going on before you got here. So I'll be glad when you're gone."

"I'll be gone soon enough, but it won't be you forcing me out the door. Despite you, I'm going to fight to save this place, and I'll fight you if you get in my way."

"Doctor Crawford, please," Jessie pleaded in a scared voice.

"Stop pulling on me, Jessie, I'm not done."

"We don't need you," Pearline spat.

"You've never needed me more. But I've taken all the crap I'm going to from you, your brother, and anybody else that's got a problem with me."

"Shayla?" Jake said.

She didn't break eye contact with Pearline. "Yes, Doctor Parker?"

"Would you go in the back with Jessie? Please," he added when she didn't move.

"I'm still doing the morning cleaning, and the patients should start arriving." The door opened and Major Spears walked in. "Right now. But Pearline and I have something to settle. No other doctor stuck around long enough to fight. But I am. You've met your match, Pearline. What you gon' do?"

"Shayla." Jake called her name, knowing that she'd finally reached the edge. They'd pushed her to the limit. Her arms were rigid, her eyes unblinking. "Shayla," he said again.

"Jake." Her voice trembled and he moved closer, not knowing if she'd fall out or cry.

"Let me handle this."

She finally looked at him, and Pearline drew in a deep breath.

Shayla's eyes were glassy and empty. She lowered her arms and the broom started to fall.

Major Spears caught it.

Jessie moved to Shayla's side and gently took her arm. "Come on, Doctor Crawford. I've got some tea in the back."

Shayla started toward the hall, but walked over to the major.

"Sir, my family greatly appreciates your part in getting me home." Shayla's halting voice tore at Jake. "I said good-bye to my grandmother. My—" Her voice caught. "Thank you."

Unexpectedly, she hugged him.

"You're welcome, young lady. Why don't you go in the back and take a rest?" He guided her by the shoulder to Jessie.

Tears streaked her face and she wiped them and balled her hands into fists. "Yes, sir. I think I will."

The door closed to room two and Jake heard the strains of music and the sound of Shayla's sobs.

He turned to Pearline. "What the hell is wrong with you?"

"Look, I didn't know she was gonna have a breakdown."

Dee gasped in horror. "You're crazy. Who do you think can take all the crap you dish out without feeling something?"

"Look at us!" Pearline hissed. "Brother against sister. Friend against friend. It wasn't like that before she got here. This is all her fault."

"Pearline, she hasn't hurt anybody but herself. She's been the best thing to ever happen to this center."

"I hate what she's done. And you're becoming just

like her. You're in love with her, aren't you?'' He didn't answer, but she seemed to know. ''You'll leave, too. It's just a matter of time.''

He looked at the woman who'd become his mother at twenty. He'd held Pearline back long enough. ''Had you talked to me, I would have told you that despite my love for Shayla I'm not going anywhere. But you are. You're fired.''

Pearline blinked until her eyes were too wide to close. ''What?''

''You heard me.''

''Fired? Because of her?'' she screeched.

''No, because of you.''

Dee set Pearline's purse on the counter.

''I don't know why I ever trusted you, Dee.''

''Shut up, Pearline. I still love you like a sister, but you're wrong. Dead wrong. Now go home. I'll call you in a few days.''

Pearline shouldered the large canvas bag and looked over her shoulder at Jake. ''From the moment I saw her, I knew you'd fall in love with her. She's going to take you away, one way or another.''

''If she does, it might be the best thing for all of us.''

''Come on, Pearl.'' Major Spears took her arm and guided her to the door. ''I'll see you home.''

The major helped Pearline into his car and they drove away.

''What the hell just happened?'' he asked Dee.

''Go see about Shayla.''

Jake walked to room two and knocked on the door. Jessie opened it and quietly slipped out.

Shayla sat on her rolling stool, her head resting on her arms on the exam table, a cool cloth on the back of her neck. She wasn't crying anymore. Just terribly quiet.

Jake didn't know where to begin. "Are you up to working today?" he said and immediately could have kicked himself.

"Yes."

"What you said yesterday made a lot of sense."

She lifted her head and stared at the wall. "I know she's your sister, but I'd appreciate it if you and she would give me just one day of peace. Tomorrow, but not today." Her face crumpled.

"I fired her."

Shayla's head fell back and she stared at the ceiling.

"I wish you'd let me hold you," he said.

She stood. "No, you can't comfort me. I'll be fine. Let's get to work. The faster I work, the faster I'm out of here."

Jake felt as if he'd been plunged into an icy river.

"If you need a break, don't hesitate to take as much time as you need, Doctor Crawford."

"I might make mistakes of the heart, but never in medicine." She left the room and was greeted with cheers from the children.

Jake hardly saw her for the rest of the day.

By sundown, the staff looked as if they'd survived triage.

Jessie lay across two metal chairs, her stick-size legs jutting out in front of her.

Jake walked into the waiting room, while Shayla and Dee counted money behind the counter.

"Dee, Jessie, I know you've heard about the new hospital opening. A few months ago, our funding was diverted into the new facility to get it opened faster. That means unless we experience a miracle, this facility will close down."

"So, it's true?" Jessie sat up. "What are we going to do?"

"Jessie, don't be so afraid. It's time for you to concentrate on your future."

"What future?"

"Medical school."

"I can't go without money!"

"There are scholarships, Jessie. You would qualify in a heartbeat."

The room fell silent. "Do you think I can make it?"

Jake tipped up her chin. "We all know you can."

"Well, what about Dee? And you? What will you do?"

"Don't worry about me. Dee is a great office manager. I'll make sure she lands on her feet."

"Jake," Dee admonished, "you can't support me and my kids. I've got to figure something out."

Shayla guided a chair behind Dee's legs and she sat.

"We're going to keep pushing to get the funding," Shayla told her, a reassuring hand on Dee's shoulder.

"What happened, Jake? How can they close us down? Your grandfather wouldn't ever have approved of this."

Jake felt as empty as the words he was about to say. "He must have changed his mind. I'm still trying to sort everything out, but I didn't want you to hear this from someone else."

"What about the money, Jake? We raised a lot, didn't we?" Dee asked.

"Yes, and that'll get us through the next few months. But I wanted you both to know. With Pearline gone, we'll have a few extra weeks, but that's it unless something else comes up."

Dee and Jessie shared the same grim expression.

"Ladies, don't worry until we give you the word that it's time. We're still working on things and Jake has a good attorney looking over the documents."

"I need this job," Jessie moaned. "It's all I have."

The meltdown was complete with both staff members

ready to cry. Jake took Jessie's hands. "Did you hear Doctor Crawford?"

She nodded slowly. "How can you save something nobody cares about?"

"People care. We just have to find them."

He caught Shayla's look and hoped he sounded reassuring.

"But the mayor promised he'd help us. What happened?"

"Come on, ladies. It's been a long day. Go home and don't worry."

They all worked as a somber quartet, cutting off lights and gathering their belongings. Shayla reached for the garbage just as Jake did. "I've got it," he said, but she pulled the bag away.

"No, I'll take care of it."

She brushed past him and accidentally bumped into Jessie. The girl winced. "I'm sorry," Shayla said, and dropped the bag.

"You've been holding that arm all day. Let me have a look."

Before Jessie could object, Shayla had rolled up her sleeve and was staring at a mean purple bruise.

"Pierce again?"

Jessie yanked her arm back. "Last time. I filed for divorce and when he found out, he twisted my arm. I'm living with Dee. If I don't have this job, I don't have anything."

Jake drew her into his arms. "You're going to medical school. We'll work this out."

Jessie cried softly as they walked outside. "Wait here, Jessie," Dee said. "Jake, talk to her."

Thunder crackled overhead.

Shayla and Dee walked the trash around back and

Shayla tossed it in. Dee started her car and rolled down the window.

"How are we going to get out of this mess?" Dee asked her.

"Where there's a will, there's a way. My grandmother used to say that."

Dee considered a moment and came to a decision. "I think I'll believe in your grandma. She did a fine job with you. Oh, a lady named Lauren called. I asked if she wanted an appointment and she said no, she just wondered how her baby was."

"My mother."

"I figured. I offered to call you, but she said you would call when you were ready; then she thanked me and hung up. She sounded worried."

"That's Mom," Shayla added after a sigh.

"You've been very good for us, Doctor Crawford."

Shayla swallowed her tears. "Thank you. Good night, Dee."

She ran around the back of the center, and Dee's headlights shone on her as Jessie climbed in.

"Shayla?" Jake called. "Wait up. I'll walk you."

"I'm fine." She sprinted ahead of him, her flashlight bouncing off the uneven forest floor.

The center's predicament had weighed heavily on her all day.

She'd run so many scenarios through her mind her head hurt, but had come up with only one conclusion.

The Crawfords would have to step in.

Jake would die, but what could he say? The needs of the people were greater than his.

Twenty-four

Simon James Bierson, Esq., had been the Parker family attorney for as long as Jake could remember. The statesman's weathered brown skin, snow-white hair, and wire-rimmed glasses were no different today from those of twenty years ago.

His eyes were the only thing that had changed. They were rheumy, and they leaked. But law hadn't seeped away like the tears that always streaked his cheeks. Simon was as astute at eighty-five as he'd been the first day Jake had met him.

"Your grandfather was a fool. Twenty years ago I told him not to deed the state his land. It's been in the Parker family for over one hundred fifty years."

Disappointment punched Jake in the stomach. "So they own it free and clear."

"I seem to recall there being more to this, but I don't have anything else in his file. We could go to court. Claim he was senile. Hell, I could testify to that." Bierson's big voice scratched against Jake's eardrum like a buzz saw. "Funny, this deed is different from the lake land."

The older man consulted a weathered map on his wall, held together by aged paper and Scotch tape. "Lookey here. That cagey old coot."

Mr. Bierson started laughing.

"What do you see?"

"One-quarter acre of the land the hospital is being built on belonged to your grandfather and now you." He nodded and pulled out a protractor and followed the measurements. "Sure do. They have to access your land to get onto their property."

"Can't they just build another entrance?"

"Sho," he agreed, wiping his cheek with a damp tissue. "But in the meantime, we gon' charge them a handsome sum to drive them tractors onto your land to get to theirs."

"That's right! I'll fight them." Jake felt conviction deep in his heart. "I've lived there all my life. They can't just steal it like candy from Deitrich's store. That land belongs to me." The angry stream of words poured out of Jake in a flood. He hated what this was doing to him. Hated that he might lose what his family had preserved for decades. And he was tired.

Tired of the helplessness that consumed him each and every time he stepped out of the center and walked home. He'd look at the lake that had never, ever run dry, and would be taken back to his childhood, and the experiences he'd hoped to share with his sons and daughters.

"File an injunction," Jake told the attorney. "Get a cease and desist order or something," he rattled, not knowing what to tell Bierson. Jake paced the room, feeling caged. "And charge them ten thousand dollars a day to access that land."

The lawyer smiled. "You got the fire, boy. But hold on, Jake. As far as this contract goes, it's lock, stock, and barrel tight. We could sue, but we'd only be wasting your money and the court's time."

"Then what the hell can I do? I came to you for a plan, not a death sentence."

"You own more land. Why not build your medical facility on that?"

"Because, Simon, where I am is where the patients know to come. We've been there for sixty years. No, that's the land I want and that's what I'll have. I don't know what Grandfather was thinking. I can't explain it. But I know he never gave anything away. Neither will I."

"There's more to this," Bierson said, flipping through the file. "But I just don't have it. I was the only black attorney in these parts for many years, so I handled everybody's business. Unless Raleigh went to Feinstein or Greenberg, I have every legal document he ever signed."

"Would he have gone to them?"

Simon merely shrugged. "Back then the races didn't mix much, but Raleigh was a different animal. He related to people as people. I'd check," he offered with a shrug.

"I feel like he didn't trust me. I was still young when he passed. Sixteen," Jake explained, still at a loss about his grandfather's actions. His emotions knocked on pity's door, but Jake forced himself not to walk into the dim gray depths. "I did all the right things."

"Don't beat yourself up, Jacob. I knew Raleigh. He always had a plan. In 1944, our army unit, unit 2221, received a letter offering a limited number of Negroes the opportunity to enter into white units fighting on the front line. You'd have to take a rank reduction to private first class, but we'd see action."

Jake had heard this story before, but for some reason, Simon Bierson's perspective dragged him to the front line and into a bunker beside his grandfather. "Twenty-five hundred of us reported, your grandfather the highest-ranking officer in our unit."

"I never knew that."

"There's a lot your grandfather never said about himself. Humble, he was. We trained in France, and Raleigh was hard on us. He wouldn't stand for us to be as good as the other men, we had to be better. Even still, many of the men were sent back to support units. Six Negroes were deployed with the rest of the white soldiers. Three of the six from Alberta. Old Elihu Weiss is still over on Porter Street, I believe. We were under tremendous fire and Raleigh saved Weiss's life. Lost his leg for his bravery. That brought the races together here in Alberta."

Jake had never met Elihu Weiss. He'd known of only one person with the last name of Weiss, and she was white. "Any relation to Barbara Weiss?"

"His granddaughter, I believe."

"She was in my class for a semester in high school and then she left."

"I'd heard her mother moved away with the girl. Old Elihu's been under the care of a caretaker for some time."

"Was he seriously injured?"

"His mind was never the same after the war. I was honored when President Clinton gave me the Bronze Star. And I know you were proud to receive your grandfather's in his honor, so you can't give up. You are Raleigh Parker's grandson. Now," Simon said, slipping the memory back into its rightful place, "we have to strategize."

"Why would Grandfather own land way over there?" Jake wondered aloud.

"Because that's how long they've been talking about building that hospital. He bought one acre."

Jake shook his head. His grandfather was a very smart man.

"If I liquidate my assets, I can buy the land next to mine and build my own medical center."

"You know how much land costs these days, Jacob? Plenty," Simon told him. "Talk to Weiss. I get over to see the old guy once a month, and most times he's lucid. Good to see you, Jake."

Jake left the attorney's office and drove directly to Feinstein's, then Greenberg's office. Neither had ever done business with his grandfather. They told great stories, wonderful tales, and wished Jake well, but couldn't help him.

He tried to see Mr. Weiss, but was told he was resting. The nurse promised to deliver a message and Mr. Weiss would get back to Jake when he could.

Discouraged, Jake drove back to his neck of the woods, twilight casting summer colors across the sky. He knew exactly where his land began and where it ended. At one time or another he had walked every inch of it.

His grandfather would never have given it away. Never. And Jake wasn't going to allow it to be stolen from him.

Twenty-five

Shayla hung up from talking to Kris, pleased.

Of course she'd had to prove that she was indeed Lauren Michaels's daughter, but once the shock wore off, Kris loved the idea of a benefit concert.

They'd hashed out details, but Shayla stopped short of a commitment. She still needed to talk to her family. She dialed the two people her mother was closest to regarding business and got both Tracey and Trisha on the phone. "What's up, Shay?" Tracey asked.

"I wanted to run something by you."

"Sure," they said together, sounding more like twins than first cousins.

"First, how've you been?" Tracey asked.

"Good." Hearing their voices made her yearn for her family and the comfort their numbers provided. There, she wasn't an outsider but part of a clan. "I'm getting better," she told them. "Still miss her, though."

"One day good memories will ease the pain of the

past few months." Trisha had always been the voice of reason. But beneath that calm veneer was a barracuda. That's why she was Lauren's road manager.

"Well," Shayla began, "the reason I wanted to speak to you two is that the center I work at is going to be closing down."

"Hallelujah! Right? Aren't you glad?" Tracey demanded. "I heard this place is a dot in the center of nowhere."

"Shut up, Tracey," Trisha said wisely. "Let the girl talk."

"It is quaint." Shayla looked at the mousetraps in the kitchen and living-room corners. "And rustic." Wind whistled from beneath the front door and Shayla used her toe to push the towel to block the draft.

But pretty pictures hung on her walls from the children and all her experiences came flooding back. "It kind of grows on you."

"So what do you need from us?" Tracey asked.

"The people we serve are moderate to low income. A new hospital is being built, but it's over forty miles away and the funding for this center has been redirected to cover costs so that hospital opens on time."

"Isn't funding allocated the year before?" Trisha wanted to know.

"It is, but when the war broke out, local governments were granted more power to delegate money where it was needed and the funds were redirected. The government wants the new facility to be finished by early next year so it can act as a primary hospital for the state in case of biological warfare. Those are good goals, but it hurts a major portion of the existing patients."

"How can we help?" Tracey's sympathetic tone reminded Shayla of why she loved being a Crawford. "Do you need donations, fund-raisers, or lobbyists?"

Shayla began hesitantly. "What we need is something big. Very big."

"You're thinking Lauren Michaels big, am I catching your drift?"

"Yes, Trish. First"—Shayla tensed as guilt wormed through her—"how is she?"

"She's as good as can be expected. Concerned that you haven't called."

"I was going to call," she tried to explain. "You don't know how isolated it is up here, but I can't. I'd be too homesick afterward."

"I hear you," Trisha said. "In your situation, you just want to get through it. Not spend all your time crying."

Like now. Shayla wiped tears from her eyes. "Do you think she's up to something like this?"

"Not sure, Shayla. She'd vowed to take six months off to deal with Chaney's affairs. And I know for a fact she just got started. Ann and Terra went with her to Chaney's house a couple weeks ago, and they said she broke down."

"I should be there with her." Shayla couldn't control her sudden tears. She sniffed and tried to stop the sob that tore out of her. "I'd been so focused on my own situation." Her thoughts turned to Jake. "I didn't think about the fact that my mother's best friend is gone. Guys, sorry I got you up so late. Forget everything I said. I'm coming home."

"Whoa," Tracey broke in. "Shayla, you can't do one thing for your mother but finish what you started in Mississippi. Remember when you came back a week after starting at the center?"

"Yeah, why?"

"The next day, a family meeting was called because my dad and the uncles were going to have it out with your father for sending you to that hellhole."

"You exaggerate so much," Shayla said, not believing what she was hearing. Crickets chirped in the silence. "You're kidding, right?"

"Tracey, I swear, your mouth is as big as your head," Trisha snapped. "Shayla, your mother needs to get back out there and feel the love people have for her. She needs to be needed right now. She wanders around looking for things to do, but we've done everything for her."

"She's a busybody. That's how she thinks things through." Although she was trying to help, Shayla still felt awful. She wasn't even home to get on her mother's nerves. She was a terrible daughter.

"You can't tell my mother or any of the aunts that," Tracey said, a note of resignation in her voice.

"They're regular butt-iners. Thank God Jade hasn't turned into one of them. I'll tell you what." Trisha flipped pages as she talked. "Lauren's schedule is open, but I need time to organize a crew, the musicians, backup, buses, insurance, et cetera. How's three weeks from Sunday?"

"That fast?" Excitement whisked through her like a Chicago wind. "Wait! I have to talk to my contact at the mayor's office just to verify the date."

"Great. I'll introduce this to your mother, or do you—"

"I do," Shayla finished. "It's time to reconnect, so to speak. Tracey?"

"Yep?"

"I need you to talk to Uncle Mike. See if he's come up with anything regarding that deed Jake's grandfather signed."

"Done," Tracey said. "Shay?"

"Yes?"

"Why are you doing this?"

Shayla had thought long and hard about her reasons. "At first I thought it was just to help the people I've gotten to know." Butterflies danced in her stomach when she thought of Jake. She wished he were with her right now. "I guess I saw a challenge and decided to go for it."

"Spoken like a true Crawford," Trisha said. "We'll talk soon."

The phone rang five times, and Shayla was afraid her mother wasn't home.

"Hello?"

"Mom," she said softly, "it's me."

"Sweetheart, how are you?"

Lauren's love came through the phone and washed Shayla in warmth. "I'm fine. I'm sorry I haven't called. I just needed time to deal with Grandma's death myself. I knew if I stayed home, you'd worry about me. Goodness knows I don't want the family to have a meeting."

"I understand," Lauren said.

A giggle tickled Shayla's ear. "How are you? Are you getting any rest?"

"Not one bit," her mother said drolly. "Honey, you know how your father and his family are."

Shayla did know. "I miss Grandma."

"Me, too. Me, too."

They each sighed, caught up in their private memories. *We're so much alike,* Shayla thought.

"How's Damon? Start any fires? Given you a new hairdo lately?"

"Don't say bad things about my little angel. He's fine. Missing you. He and Daddy are out digging for worms. They're going fishing."

"Mom, it's freezing outside."

"Honey, Damon doesn't care."

Shayla took a deep breath. "I'm almost scared to ask, but how is Daddy?"

"Going nuts, of course." This time her mother's giggle was sneaky. "If he talks to Dee one more time, I think he'll know how many hairs are on her head. He's called every day."

"Dee never said a word."

"He asked her not to." Her mother's tone turned worried. "Sweetheart, are you sure you're okay? You sound so tired."

"Mom." Shayla rested her head on her hand. "Life is something else when you finally grow up."

Laughter filled her ears. "Really, darling? I had no idea."

"You're cute, lady. I was so spoiled."

"I never noticed any spoiled behavior."

"Mom, I can't believe you'd lie like that. You had your hand in the making of this monster, so own up. I think you have more Ferragamo shoes than I do."

"I like Jimmy Choo."

Shayla giggled. "How could you stand me? I was an absolute terror. Dressed very nicely, I might add, but awful."

"That's all your dad's fault. You were a good girl, and then your dad and his family started throwing money, cars, and expensive toys at you. I used to think they had a secret tunnel to Fort Knox. Here I was with my hundred-thousand-dollar portfolio, thinking I'm doing something, and then your father walks into our lives, and out of his pocket he pulls Emory University. Honey, I took my little hundred grand and buried it in a cave."

"Called Microsoft," Shayla threw in.

"You do have a good memory," her mother said, impressed. "Your dad was something back then and he's something else now that my singing career has bloomed. I still don't understand how one family could have dentists, doctors, judges, ambassadors, *and* a bounty hunter."

"She married in. You can't count her," Shayla added. "How are Nick and Jade?"

"Adorable now that she's expecting."

"Oh my goodness," Shayla cried, missing everyone even more. "I bet Nick's beside himself."

"Shayla." Her mother's voice dropped to a whisper. "He's got morning sickness."

This sent them into a fit of giggles. "Oh, Mom."

"Looking forward to coming back?" her mom asked.

"Yes," she said softly, unable to tell her she just wanted the right reason to stay.

"Your office looks wonderful."

"Tracey told me."

"You've talked to your cousin?" her mother asked, trying not to sound wounded.

Shayla rushed to reassure her. "Not really. Actually, we were talking about you."

"Darling, I'm going to be fine. I have my moments when I'm strong . . ." Lauren's voice faded. "But there are times when I can't stand Mom not being just a phone call away. I'm better though. I've only cried once today."

"Should I come home?" All the guilt that had dissipated returned in a flood. Her mother hadn't said the words, but she needed to touch her daughter. Shayla could feel it in her bones. Distance hadn't broken that bond.

"No, you have work to do. I'll be fine. I think I'm going back to work next month."

"Are you up for it?"

"Yes!" Her mom laughed. "This house is too big for me and Damon. He's got stuff everywhere. All I do is clean up and I'm sure your father wonders what I've been up to all day."

"Please. He's a terrible housekeeper. Damon isn't even a good excuse. Mom," she said before she lost her nerve, "I need a favor."

"Is it money?"

"No! Gosh, give me some credit."

"You need my credit card, then."

Shayla laughed. "I had that coming. I know my hand's been out for the past few years and you and Daddy have been more than generous."

"Honey, are you paying us back for all the money you borrowed?"

"No way! I'm reformed, not crazy."

Her mother got a good laugh out of that. "I can't help but tease you, I'm sorry. What do you need?"

"The state has redirected funding for the center to a new facility, and the people we serve won't get medical care. They're wonderful people who just don't have a lot."

Shayla talked about Rosalie, and the women at her church and the patients who benefited from their care. And she talked about Jake.

"It sounds like a wonderful place."

"It is. This is probably the biggest favor I've ever asked for."

"I'm listening," Lauren said.

"We're going to have to close in a few weeks if we don't get funding. Feel free to say no, but I wish you'd take a few days and think about it. I'd like for you to please, please consider doing a benefit concert." Shayla bothered her furrowed forehead. "In three weeks. I know this probably costs a fortune, and I should have taken better care over the years to realize how much work is involved, but I'm all grown up now and I won't be disappointed if you say no. I'll understand, really. So if you could please just give it some thought, please think about it—"

"Yes."

Shayla stopped talking. "You said yes."

"I said yes. Honey, call Trisha with the details. I can't wait to meet Dee and Jessie and Jake."

They both gasped at a loud crash. "Your brother's inside. I've got to run. Love you, darling."

"Mom, don't hang up!"

"What is it?"

"Thank you," she said in a rush. "I love you. This is fantastic. Thank you. I love you, Mom."

"I know. Bye, darling."

Twenty-six

Jake hadn't heard from Elihu Weiss by midweek and had started thinking he'd never hear from the man. His nurse had been playing offensive tackle and Jake wasn't getting anywhere.

In the meantime, he'd searched high and low for additional legal documents, but had found nothing.

Just when Jake thought he was without options, the phone rang and Mr. Weiss told Jake to be at his house at ten A.M. sharp.

Jake rushed out of the center door and straight into Shayla.

"Sorry," he said as he plowed into her.

"Where's the fire?"

These were the first words she'd spoken to him since they'd made love. Jake couldn't define how much he'd missed her. He knew he just didn't want to let her go. His body felt as if he found something he'd been missing. "Is someone hurt?" she asked.

Me. "No, I've got an appointment with a man who knew my grandfather very well. I don't know. He might know something. Maybe not. We'll see." Jake stepped back. "I don't need to trouble you with this."

Her eyes raked him. "It's no trouble."

"Has your uncle come up with anything?"

Sadly, Shayla shook her head. "No, he hasn't called. He's on my list to call tonight."

"Don't bother him. If you haven't heard from him now, he didn't find anything."

"Still not willing to admit you need help, huh?" She stepped close and kissed him squarely on the lips. "How's it feel way up there next to God?"

Jessie burst out onto the steps. "Oh my goodness! I just heard on the radio that Lauren Michaels is doing a benefit concert here in Alberta, Mississippi, for our center."

Jake's brows wrinkled. "I don't know anything about that."

"Dee heard it, too." Jessie was grinning from ear to ear. "Lauren said she heard about our plight, and she's giving one hundred percent of the proceeds to the Alberta Medical Center. Can you believe it? Do you remember her song 'Silken Love'? Oh my goodness." Jessie grew starry-eyed.

Jake still couldn't believe what she was saying. "I'd better call Kris and see what's going on."

"Don't forget your ten o'clock." Shayla stepped around Jake and walked inside.

He raced down the stairs and into his truck. With five minutes to spare, he arrived outside the residence of Elihu Weiss, his nerves stretched to the limit.

What the hell was going on?

Up until he'd met Shayla, his life had followed a

steady course, never deviating far from work and home. Now he faced losing everything.

Pearline wasn't speaking to him, his land was a step away from being taken, he was nearly out of a job, and he was in love with a woman who would be leaving soon.

So why was he being granted a guardian angel like Lauren Michaels? Either fate had a sick sense of humor, or there were forces at work around him he didn't know about.

He exited the truck and walked up outdated stone steps that fit well into the well-maintained home. The exterior of the plantation-style home was pristine, reminiscent of a time gone by.

Jake rang the doorbell, the musical chime vibrating throughout the vast halls.

A minute later, the door opened and an elderly man stood in the doorway. "Raleigh?"

"No, I'm Jake Parker, Raleigh's grandson."

"Why don't you come in," a female voice said. Jake then noticed a casually dressed black woman, a warm smile on her face. "I'm Esse, Mr. Weiss's caretaker. How do you do, Doctor Parker?"

"Fine. Pleasure to meet you."

Weiss scuttled around from the left, then right. "Mr. Weiss, it's a pleasure to meet you, too."

He looked up at Jake through his glasses and shook his hand vigorously. "Of course. Aren't you a doctor?"

Jake grinned. "Yes, sir."

Weiss started down the hall and then turned and waved to Esse.

"Go on, I've got company. I've got a visitor, so you go on."

Esse smiled at her boss. "He's very excited. He doesn't get much company. His friends have all passed away or are too ill to visit. He forgets sometimes. Past and present blend into the same conversation. But if you take things at his pace, you'll be fine.''

"I understand."

She pulled on a light jacket. "I'll just be next door if you need me."

"That's fine. We'll wait for you to return."

"Go on, Esse. You're stealing my visitor. Come this way," Weiss told Jake. Jake followed the man on a journey through a house that reflected an old life. Everything had been maintained from the first half of the 1900s, all the way down to the lace doilies on the armchairs. As he expected, the house gleamed with the shininess of a new penny.

The stooped man bustled with unexpected energy, although he had a slight lift in his hip. At the end of the hallway, he turned around and returned to the front where they settled in a drawing room, a sterling silver tea set between them. "Have some tea?"

"No, thank you, sir. I just wanted to ask you a question about my grandfather."

"Raleigh?"

"Yes, sir."

Elihu sat back, his big-boned knuckles pressing through thin skin. "Raleigh had a nice daughter. You ever met her?"

"Yes, sir," Jake said. "She was my mother."

"Oh," he said gently. "You're Raleigh's grandson. You got so big. You used to tell me you were all growed up. I used to laugh." He laughed now, as did Jake. "Well, what did you want to ask me?"

"Did Grandfather ever tell you anything about his land?"

"Raleigh liked to buy land," Weiss said with authority. "I told him to invest in the stock market, but the crash spooked him. He said land was forever." A long pause fell between them. "When we were in the army, I couldn't get enough of your chili. How's your leg? You took a load of shrapnel for me, friend. I'll never forget that."

Jake's heart pounded at the sincerity in Weiss's eyes.

"What can I do for you, good friend?"

"I'm Jake Parker. Raleigh's grandson."

"Did you come for your grandfather's mail? Raleigh doesn't come by the way he used to. Leg must be bothering him." He grew sad. "Took a load of shrapnel. I came home with a broken nose. This old hip wasn't replaced until the seventies. Can hardly call that a war injury. Some veteran I turned out to be."

"No, sir. My grandfather was very proud to call you his friend. You gave him comfort over in France knowing someone from home was looking out for him. He always said, 'Had things been different, Weiss would have done the same for me.' "

"Righty-o about that. Loved that bony man like a brother."

Weiss pushed the top back on his antique rolltop desk and pulled out a packet of papers and three letters.

"Raleigh was supposed to come for these a couple weeks ago, but I guess getting around in his truck is taking a toll with his leg and all."

Weiss stared with wanderlust out the window over his garden.

Although the summer flowers were gone, someone had planted hundreds of pansies. "Wish he'd come by. I had the ramp installed for him."

Jake looked around, but didn't see signs of a ramp or even a recent visitor. Mr. Weiss's worlds were intermixed and would probably stay that way until he died.

"What's going on with the war? Have the Vietcong given up?" Weiss asked.

"No," Jake lied. "They're still fighting."

"Esse said the same thing yesterday. Looks nice outside. Good day for a walk."

Life and time had passed this man by, but he was Jake's grandfather's friend. Jake couldn't stand by even with his troubles and not give Elihu Weiss a few more minutes of his time.

"When was the last time you checked on your garden?"

"Just yesterday. I recall that I finished watching Carter give his inauguration speech and went outside. Course it was dark. But can you believe a Democrat is going to be president? I can't go outside without Esse. She gets mighty upset if I leave her. She needs a walk every day to clear her mind."

Jake chuckled. "Would you like to go outside with me? We could stop next door and let Esse know we're out."

Weiss's face lit up. "I'll get my sweater. Do you need a sweater?" he called from the hall closet.

"No, thank you." Jake picked up his grandfather's discarded mail and papers.

At first glance, he could tell they were important. Suddenly a calm stole over him.

Jake would take Mr. Weiss on his first walk outside in almost twenty years, then get to the papers.

Three hours later Jake sprinkled headache powder into water and stirred before drinking. Elihu Weiss had been full of information, not all consistent, but bits had triggered memories in Jake he hadn't expected.

He'd made the connection with Mr. Weiss halfway through their walk. Raleigh had never called him by his full name, but Eli. They'd been friends, when black and white men were on opposite sides of the race fight.

The mail from Weiss sat on the table and Jake stared at the thirty-year-old envelopes. He lifted the first letter and slit it open, the legal mumbo jumbo aggravating his already throbbing head.

A knock rattled his door.

"Where've you been?" Pearline asked after coming in.

Jake dropped a dish towel over the letters and moved to the living room where she went.

"Visiting. Why?"

"I stopped by earlier and you weren't here. So, how'd you manage to get Lauren Michaels to agree to a benefit concert?"

Jake rubbed his tired eyes and sat on the solid-wood coffee table in front of his sister. "What are you doing here?"

"You never used to ask me why I was coming to visit."

"You were never as mean as you've been lately."

"She's the cause."

"Pearline, you know better. You're acting worse than a child."

"You fired me."

"You deserved it. God, I have a headache. You should have known I'd never do anything to hurt you."

The defiant scowl dropped from Pearline's face. She shrugged. "I can't work with her."

Jake reached for his sister. "Pearline, I—"

Her eyes filled. "I knew you'd fall in love with her." Pearline pushed to her feet. "The major and I are going away for the weekend."

"What?" Jake asked, surprised.

"We thought we might see if we could get along."

They stood at the door, so much unsaid between them.

"Well, I'm happy for both of you."

"Thanks. I hope you know what you're doing," Pearline told Jake.

He nodded. "I have no idea what I'm doing, but I think I'll ride it out."

Pearline threw her arms around him. "Figure it out before you make a big mistake."

"You too. Have a good weekend."

"Thanks."

Jake walked over to the phone and dialed Kris.

Kris waved at her sparse committee of two who'd come by to plan Lauren Michaels's visit to Alberta. Ticket sales were brisk and the mayor's office was fielding calls from Mississippi's elite who wanted special seats. For the first time ever, Kris was glad to tell them all seats were on a first-come, first-serve basis.

They'd get no special treatment for this event.

Shayla and Alice King heeded Kris's warning and quieted.

"Jake," Kris said, "no, I don't know Lauren Michaels. I don't know any more than you. I heard she heard about the center's situation and wanted to help. No, I'm not lying. That's how I heard about it. Have you taken care of all your business?" She nodded. "Fine. Talk soon. Bye." She hung up. "I don't know how long you can keep your mother's identity a secret."

Shayla grew antsy. "That was part of the agreement. Jake can't know." They both gave her odd looks. "At least not now. Jake couldn't handle it. The less he knows the better."

"She's in love with him," Kris told Alice.

"I remember that feeling," the older woman said. "You should be honest with him."

"He can't even accept what he sees. He thinks I'm silk and lace and very expensive leather," she said as she fingered the gloves her mother had given her for Christmas. "But I play in dirt and I drink beer from a bottle and I even eat at fast-food restaurants." Shayla fought back unexpected tears. "And I shop at Wal-Mart. And my mother is Lauren Michaels. And my father is Doctor Eric Crawford. Jake can't handle the truth. What he doesn't know would probably kill him." Shayla stood and pulled her mustard-colored leather coat over her right arm.

Kris handed Shayla her portfolio. "Then what's it all for?"

"For everybody here who needs help and can't afford it." Shayla shrugged. "The people need this center. They need Jake. Even if he can't love me for who I am, I know where his heart is, and that's something I can do something about."

"Then you walk away?" Alice asked.

"My father is expecting me to report to his practice in two months. They remodeled my office," she added lamely. "Look, I'll fax all this to Trisha tonight and we'll keep in touch. Promise me you won't tell him."

"Promise," they said together.

Shayla stood at the door. "It's what he wants. Good night."

Shayla walked into work Monday and hurried to the fax machine. She quickly sent the documents to Trisha and had gathered them up when Jake walked in.

"Good morning, Doctor Parker." She headed to

room two and shoved the papers in her purse. "You're early."

"Had to fax something. Seems you did too."

"Yes," she said, closing the door on his unasked question. "How did your meeting go with Mr. Weiss?"

"I'm glad my grandfather had such a good friend. He's been holding mail for my grandfather for thirty years. I tried to read through it, but the mumbo jumbo is . . . I'm a doctor," he said, giving up. "I'm going to fax it to Simon and see what he says."

"He was your grandfather's attorney, right?"

"Right."

"Why not give my uncle a shot at them, too? He wouldn't mind. If it turns out to be nothing, then you haven't lost anything."

Jake shook his head. "I don't want to bother him."

"No bother at all. Here." She took the papers from his hand and walked to the machine. "I'll send them over, and who knows? You might get lucky."

Shayla was more reserved than he'd ever seen her. She moved efficiently, sending the documents and then returning them to the envelope. She headed back to room two.

She stood in the center of the small space, her arms crossed over her chest. "What is it, Jake?"

"Shayla, what's going on?"

"Nothing."

"Do you have anything to do with Lauren Michaels coming here?"

"Why do you ask such questions when you know that's not what I want to talk about?"

His eyes widened.

"Do you care for me, Jake?"

"You know I do."

"Love me?"

"Yes, in my own way I do, Shayla."

"But you're willing to walk away from me."

"Yes. I have to stay here."

She stood in front of him. "I respect a man with convictions."

Jake took Shayla in his arms and let his lips encompass hers. Their tongues met in a gentle tangle that sparked a groundswell of emotion that urged Jake closer to her.

He wanted her, couldn't imagine being without her, but again his choices threatened to dampen his passion. Shayla was the woman for him. But his simple cabin and meager salary would soon disappear. Then he'd have even less to offer than when they'd first met. He started to let her go.

"Don't say good-bye to me just yet," she whispered.

Jake swept her in his arms and deepened their kiss. He could hardly deny her.

Twenty-seven

Jake walked around the music hall, amazed that every seat was filled with people eager to see Lauren Michaels.

All week the patients had been abuzz with talk, the excitement escalating, until even Jake couldn't help but become excited.

TV crews had turned up to interview him and the staff, the same question coming from different reporters. Why had Lauren Michaels decided to help them?

Jake still didn't know. Several times he'd tried to ask Shayla, and Jessie and Dee, but nobody had any more answers than he.

Shayla had been cool all week, avoiding being alone with him, but then she'd surprise him with a gentle touch or a long, thoughtful look. But she'd kept her distance, so that by the end of the week, Jake yearned for her so deeply he could hardly think straight.

How could he stand to let her go?

He pulled out the ticket couriered to the center in

the middle of the week. Dee, Jessie, Shayla, and he had been invited to the concert as Lauren Michaels's special guests.

Jake showed his badge to the tight backstage security team and was taken to the greenroom. He'd been told he would meet Ms. Michaels before the show, if she had time, and that alone made him nervous.

He'd loved her ballads, had fallen in love when "Right Now" sailed to the top of the charts, but he'd never imagined, not in his wildest dreams, meeting the woman who'd been responsible for so many people falling in love.

Jake walked into the greenroom, unable to believe the place actually existed. He'd always thought the greenroom was a showbiz myth, but as he sank into one of the captain's chairs and turned on his personal television set, Jake couldn't help but admire the first-class treatment. Who wouldn't enjoy this?

He leaned back until the chair was fully reclined, then scrambled to his feet when he heard voices outside the door. They faded and Jake calmed his nervousness by going over to the buffet table and selecting from the feast.

Not only was Lauren Michaels doing the center a great service, but her involvement had turned the media's focus to the treatment of the city's poor versus the city's desire for a brand-new hospital.

Because of media scrutiny, the council had amended their former plan regarding upfront payment for ambulatory services and recently announced that the members would consider opening a satellite office in the city of Alberta. Jake may have lost the fight for the land, but any money from this event would build another center, bigger and better than the one they currently had.

There'd be room for the computers Shayla had

trained the staff to use, and Jake would personally make sure cranky nurses were in every room where children were seen.

He yearned for Shayla. Needed to hold her. But she'd been elusive, her gentle touches and private winks fading with each passing day. Jake wanted to talk to her, but at the moment he didn't know where she was.

He paced the room until he was in front of the buffet table again.

A tall, brown-skinned man walked in and Jake knew right away he was a relative of Shayla's. The gray eyes gave him away. "Doctor Parker?"

Jake snatched up a napkin and wiped his hands. "Yes. I'm Doctor Parker. You're a Crawford."

"Michael, Shayla's uncle." He paused. "The attorney."

"Right," Jake said. "I'm sorry, I didn't expect to meet you here. You came all the way from Atlanta?"

Mike gave him a funny look. "I live there."

Jake didn't know what else to say. "So how'd you get back here?"

"I came with the rest of the family. Look, Doctor Parker, we don't have much time tonight, but I was able to wade through some of the papers. Your grandfather was an interesting man."

"I appreciate your time and expertise, Mr. Crawford."

"Michael."

"Michael," Jake corrected. "But my attorney said these papers were nothing but the long-winded gibberish of a man about to go insane. So thanks for all you've done, and I'd be glad to compensate you for your time."

"How does ten percent sound to you?"

"Fine. What?" Jake said. "No. I'm not giving you ten percent of nothing."

"I'd hardly call ten percent of twenty million dollars

nothing. Also, it's bad business to enter into an agreement without knowing all the facts."

Jake's head went light. "What are you talking about? Twenty million dollars? The state owns my land now."

"That's true. And for that land they owe you twenty million dollars. Your grandfather deeded this land to the state under the auspices that they not build another medical facility within one hundred miles of the current facility. If I'm correct, the new hospital is almost forty miles from your facility."

"That's true. But the city will fight this. Their attorneys don't have any knowledge of this—"

Michael Crawford smiled. "Yes, they do and they'll settle. The new hospital will be built and you will be a very rich man. Let's talk details tomorrow. Enjoy the show."

Michael Crawford exited as quietly as he came and Jake stumbled to a chair.

Twenty million dollars. *Twenty million dollars.*

He'd never even had a million quarters or dimes, or even pennies. Not at once. His chest almost burst. Jake stood and grabbed another napkin to wipe his forehead.

He could do so much with that money.

He could build a real medical facility. Not just a building that was barely big enough to service patients, but one with an elevator that led to floors. They could have a children's ward. And computers to make translation easier. And doctors like Rosalie.

Jake walked to the door and back to his seat. He wanted to talk to Shayla so badly. The money would change everything.

He stopped pacing. The money would change him.

He was already thinking of what he could do. But the land would be gone. His family's land. His legacy.

Funny how the building's paint had turned from

acceptable to drab gray when set against cold, hard cash. Jake made it to the door when Dee and Jessie were ushered in, their eyes and mouths agape.

"Jake," Jessie squealed, "this is a dream come true."

"Wow, look at all that food. Do you know we have front-row seats?" Dee walked over to the table and fixed a small plate. "Jake, you want something?"

"No," he said quietly when the door opened again. His heartbeat slammed against his chest. "Shayla."

He reached for her and she gave him a chaste kiss on the cheek.

"Are you all ready for the show?"

"Yes. I met your uncle. He had some news regarding the papers we faxed to him."

"Really?" She took his hands and squeezed. "Is there anything you want to say to me?"

Jake couldn't ask her to share her life with him now. He'd been resisting her love for months, and now that he would have money he wanted to turn the tables. He'd rejected her when he thought he couldn't provide her with "things."

Now that he'd have money, he'd want to give her the world. The only problem was, he knew she wouldn't stand for it. Shayla was richer than he'd ever be, in spirit and in love. He'd cheated himself. He'd pushed away a woman who only wanted one thing from him and that was him. Shayla wouldn't stand for it.

This was what "for richer or poorer" meant.

Would she ever question if his love was true?

Jake knew he'd cast the die by never loving Shayla for herself. "Not now," he told her. "Let's talk later. Just know—"

She held him tighter. "What, Jake?"

He wanted to commit right then. Right there. Ask her to be his wife forever. But he'd botched everything.

Used the very prejudice against her that he'd claimed to despise. Jake had no idea how to right this wrong.

"Later, baby. Please."

Shayla's hands fell away. "I have to go. Enjoy the show."

She hurried over to hug Dee and Jessie and strode out of the greenroom.

Jake watched her go and wished he could call her back.

A tall gray-eyed woman entered.

"Doctor Parker, ladies, are you ready?"

"Yes," they chimed.

"Let's go."

The concert hall rocked with excitement, the people bursting in anticipation. When the music started and Lauren Michaels came out singing, everybody left their seats and cheered.

For two hours, Lauren sang her heart out until Jake was completely won over. At the end of the show, Lauren called Jake onstage and presented him with a check that staggered him.

She acknowledged and thanked Alice King and Kris for making her trip to Alberta so comfortable. Then she thanked the citizens of Alberta for supporting the Alberta Medical Center. The crowd of every day, regular people gave her love in a lasting ovation that brought Lauren to tears.

Lauren walked on very high heels and started the song that made her famous, "Silken Love." The women in the audience screamed and Jake couldn't believe the tremendous rush of love he felt knowing the words she spoke applied to him and Shayla. Lauren walked to stage right. "Ladies and gentlemen, meet my husband, Doctor Eric Crawford!"

The women in the audience screamed, and the handsome doctor smiled, his eyes only for his wife. Jake's gut clenched.

Shayla's father.

Jake closed his eyes, but couldn't escape Lauren's next words.

"And my beautiful baby girl, Shayla Michaels-Crawford."

Twenty-eight

In the dressing room, Lauren sashayed as she walked, the long silver dress complementing her slim figure. She was still wired, pacing the floor as she did after every show. She ran her hands through her sweat-dampened hair and sipped water as she walked. "Did I sound okay?"

"You were spectacular." Shayla sat in a comfortable chair, resting her chin on her hand. They'd repeated this routine a thousand times, but tonight everything seemed to crystallize in a bubble that could pop at any second.

Lauren stopped in front of Shayla and raised her daughter's chin.

"What is it, darling?"

"Nothing."

Her mom shook her head. "If that were true, you'd have told me to stop asking you after the third time. You'd have been in my closet on the bus to see what surprises I'd brought you, and you'd have sworn never to tell your father. Now, what's the matter?"

"I need a hug." Shayla reached for her mother and was engulfed.

"Darling, you're scaring me."

Shayla wiped tears from her eyes. "I'm in love with a man who doesn't know I have dignitaries for relatives."

"If he had any sense, he'd love you just for you."

"He has plenty of sense. That's his problem, he thinks too much."

Her mom chuckled. "Why does he care who's hanging from your family tree?"

"Because he thinks he could never be enough for me. He didn't know Dad was Doctor Eric Crawford who is married to—"

"Ah." Her mother smiled, her stage makeup making her look quite glamorous. "Me."

"Right." Shayla sniffed.

"Honey, couldn't you have told him before we arrived? We *are* a bit much to the average person."

"Mom, he didn't want to love me when he *suspected* I had money. Now he knows I have money!"

Lauren giggled. "That's easy. You're cut off."

"Mom, you're not funny. What should I do?"

"Are you coming home, Shayla?"

She'd thought on this a hundred times. Shayla wanted to stay in Alberta, but only for the right reasons. Only for Jake's love.

"There's my girl." Eric Crawford entered the room and grabbed Shayla from the chair into a big hug.

She loved her father and inhaled deeply.

He looked over his daughter's shoulder to his wife. "What's wrong with my kid?"

"You should ask her, Mr. Crawford."

"I'm not seventeen anymore, I can hear you," Shayla told them as she grabbed a tissue from the box.

Her father took her mother's hand and led her to her personal chaise longue. "Why are you still on your feet? Shayla, even after all these years, she still doesn't listen. Now what's wrong with you?"

"Nothing."

"Oh, no, you don't. I didn't come all this way to be told nothing. Women are crying in here and I want to know why."

"Mom, would you please get your husband?"

"Honey, that's between you and your father. I'm just here to watch."

"Go sit by your mother."

Her father took her chair and sat down. "Do these tears have anything to do with the young man I found lurking in the hallway, insisting he needs to speak to you?"

Shayla shot to her feet and ran into the bathroom. "Don't open the door, I have raccoon eyes." She fixed her face and caught her parents exchanging a look. "Okay, Daddy. Open the door."

Eric nodded and ushered Jake in. "Doctor Jake Parker, my wife, Lauren Michaels."

Lauren swung her feet to the floor and stood. "Doctor Parker, the pleasure is mine."

"Please call me Jake. It's an honor." His gaze floated to Shayla. "Hey, baby."

A tingle slithered up Shayla's spine. "Hi."

Jake spoke to Shayla's father. "I understand you have a practice in Atlanta and are expecting your daughter to join you."

"I am."

"I hope you won't be offended if I try to change her mind."

Shayla's heart skipped a beat.

"Why would you do that, Doctor Parker?" Lauren was now standing beside her husband. "Shayla's our daughter. And I would think you'd understand that her rightful place would be with her family in our practice in Atlanta."

"I agree, but I'd like to expand the practice a little bit."

"Why would you do that?" Lauren asked.

"Because I love her."

Shayla said nothing.

Her mother's eyebrows lifted. "When did you come to this realization?"

"Yes, Jake. When did this happen? You loved me before, but you pushed me away. Do you love me now that all the leaves of my family tree look greener?"

"When I realized before I thought I had nothing that could measure up and then I really did have nothing. I was faced with no job, I'd lost my family's property, and I'd lost you. It still hadn't occurred to me that I had you until before the concert, before all of this."

"Why now, Jake?"

"I'd lost everything, but you still wanted me. Then your uncle told me a secret that could enrich my life, but I was poor because I didn't have you. I love you, Shayla."

She moved away from him. "You tormented me. You knew I loved you and you kept pushing me away."

"I'm not very smart."

Lauren and Eric giggled and Shayla sent them a withering look.

"Don't mind us," her father said, starting a CD of soothing music and pulling his wife into his arms.

Shayla watched her parents become engulfed with the love that was the backbone of their relationship.

"We'll just wait for the verdict over here," Eric said as he danced Lauren in small circles.

"How are you rich, Jake?"

"In love. In knowledge. And money."

"What?"

"The state of Mississippi owes me twenty million dollars."

"No!" Shayla's hands shot to her mouth.

"Will you marry me?"

"Wait." Shayla regarded him over her shoulder. "Repeat that."

Jake grinned. "I want you to stay."

"Oh."

"I know it'd be different from being in Atlanta and around your friends and family, but it's only a few hours away. We could visit your folks as often as you wanted."

"Oh, Jake," Shayla cried.

"They could come here," he said, taking her hands in his. "I'd build a house big enough for us and them and your little brother."

She laughed, her smile watery. He sank to one knee. "Please, Shayla Michaels-Crawford, will you marry me?"

Shayla hiked up her skirt and kneeled in front of him too.

She saw the approval in her mother's and father's eyes, but she needed to make Jake understand. "Overnight you'd become a son and a grandson, a nephew, and soon, a husband." She touched his cheek. "We are dentists and lawyers, judges and doctors, and interior designers, and bounty hunters, and karate experts, and students, and ambassadors of small countries, and the children of superstars. We're role models."

Shayla looked away. "There're lots of us, and we're not all rich, but my parents are, and from what I heard after my grandmother's funeral, I am, too. I'm spoiled,

Jake, and I love with a ferocity that's the Crawford trade-mark.''

She cupped his cheeks. ''The question is, will you marry us?''

Jake's hands reached up and held hers. He brought her close and looked directly into Shayla's eyes. His mouth touched hers.

''To all of you, yes.''

Dear Readers:

Thank you for being patient with this latest installment of the Crawford family. I heard your requests for just one more story and thought Shayla Michaels-Crawford was grown up enough to carry her own book.

If you're interested in the the previous Crawford stories, ask your bookseller to order SILKEN LOVE, KEEPING SECRETS, or ENDLESS LOVE. The Crawfords have been a wonderful family to write about. I hope you've enjoyed DOCTOR, DOCTOR. For information about my other titles, visit my Web site at www.authorcarmengreen.com or e-mail me at carmengreenl@aol.com.

Blessings,
Carmen Green

More Sizzling Romances From
Carmen Green

__**Now or Never**	0-7860-0327-8	**$4.99**US/**$6.50**CAN
__**Keeping Secrets**	0-7860-0494-0	**$4.99**US/**$6.50**CAN
__**Silken Love**	1-58314-095-6	**$5.99**US/**$7.99**CAN
__**Endless Love**	1-58314-135-9	**$5.99**US/**$7.99**CAN
__**Commitments**	1-58314-226-6	**$5.99**US/**$7.99**CAN